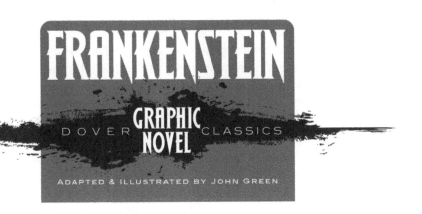

FRANKENSTEIN

DOVER GRAPHIC NOVEL CLASSICS

ADAPTED & ILLUSTRATED BY JOHN GREEN

MARY SHELLEY

D1371946

DOVER PUBLICATIONS, INC.
MINEOLA, NEW YORK

Originally written in 1818 by Mary Shelley, the story of Victor Frankenstein's monster is a compelling tale of horror. Shunned by everyone, the creature quickly turns to evil and vows retribution on Frankenstein for creating him. In *Frankenstein*, Mary Shelley succeeded in presenting a story that, as she stated in her own words, "would speak to the mysterious fears of our nature and awaken thrilling horror—one to make the reader dread to look round, to curdle the blood, and quicken the beatings of the heart."

Although the legendary story of *Frankenstein* has been abridged here, a special effort has been made to preserve the authenticity of the narrative and keep as much of the original dialogue as space allows. The evocative illustrations enable colorists to vividly bring this compelling story to life by using crayons, colored pencils, or markers.

Bibliographical Note

FRANKENSTEIN (Dover Graphic Novel Classics), first published by Dover Publications, Inc., in 2014, is a republication of the work originally published in a different format (Color Your Own Graphic Novel) by Dover in 2010.

International Standard Book Number

ISBN-13: 978-0-486-78505-9
ISBN-10: 0-486-78505-X

Manufactured in the United States by Courier Corporation
78505X02   2015
www.doverpublications.com

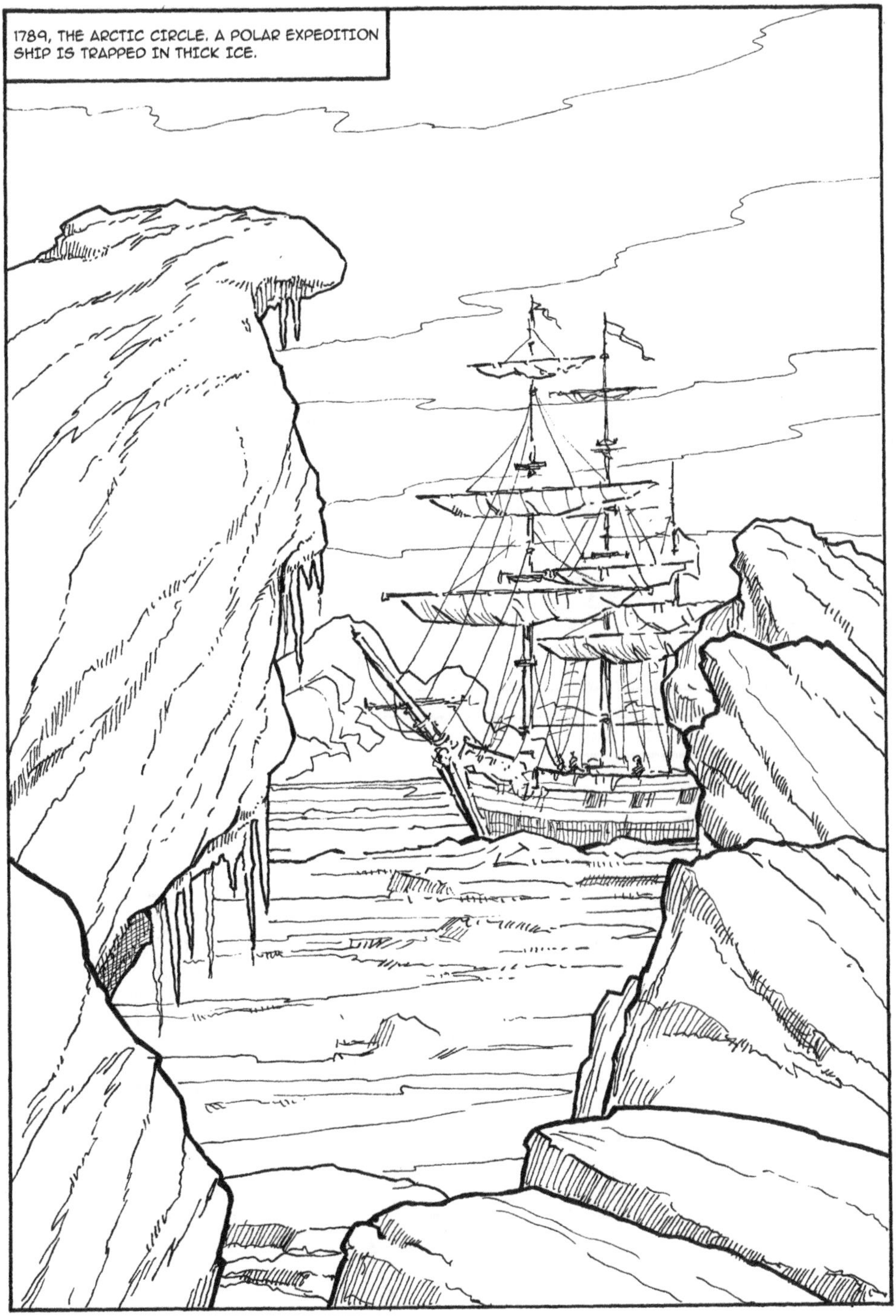
1789, THE ARCTIC CIRCLE. A POLAR EXPEDITION SHIP IS TRAPPED IN THICK ICE.

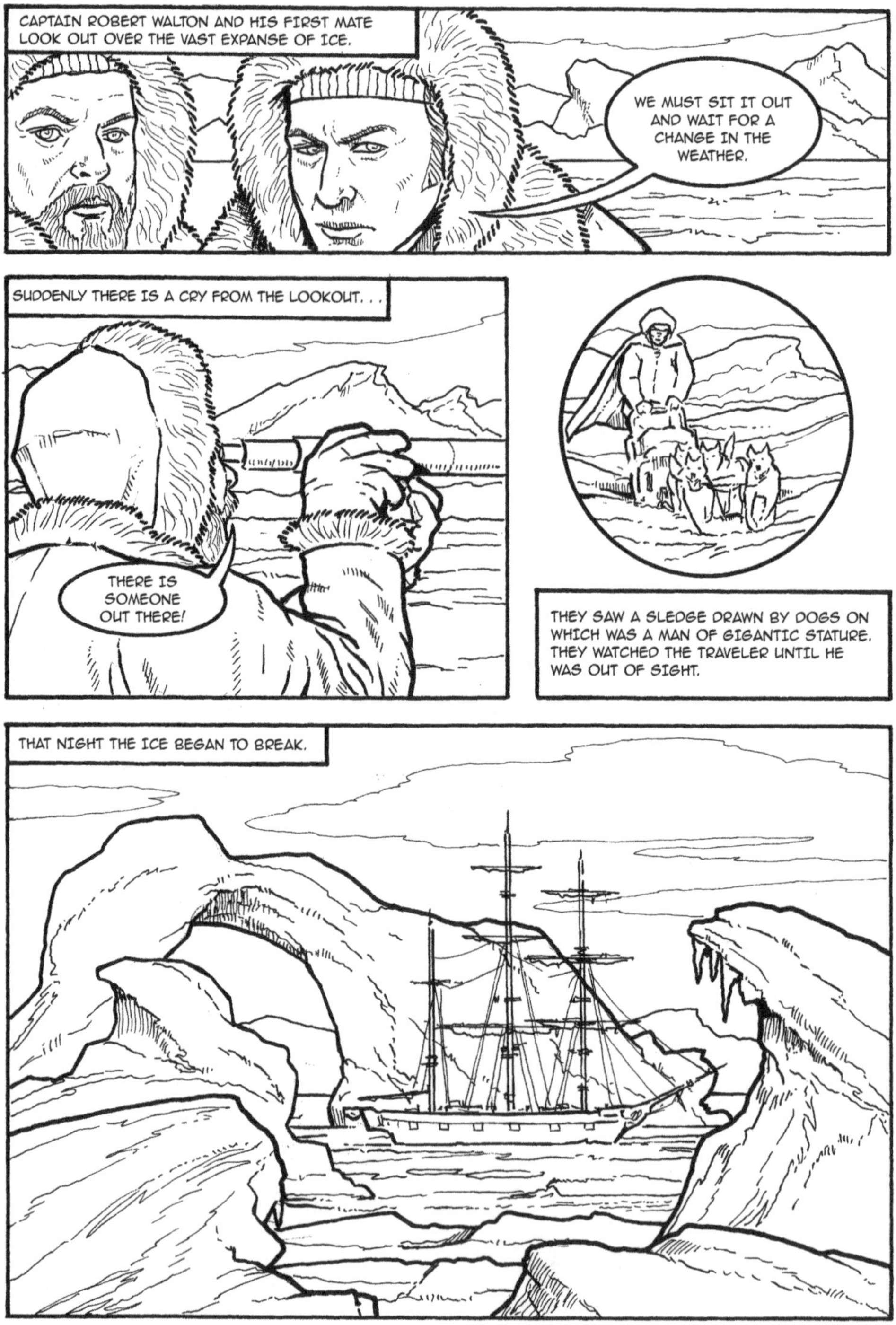
CAPTAIN ROBERT WALTON AND HIS FIRST MATE LOOK OUT OVER THE VAST EXPANSE OF ICE.
WE MUST SIT IT OUT AND WAIT FOR A CHANGE IN THE WEATHER.
SUDDENLY THERE IS A CRY FROM THE LOOKOUT. . .
THERE IS SOMEONE OUT THERE!
THEY SAW A SLEDGE DRAWN BY DOGS ON WHICH WAS A MAN OF GIGANTIC STATURE. THEY WATCHED THE TRAVELER UNTIL HE WAS OUT OF SIGHT.
THAT NIGHT THE ICE BEGAN TO BREAK.

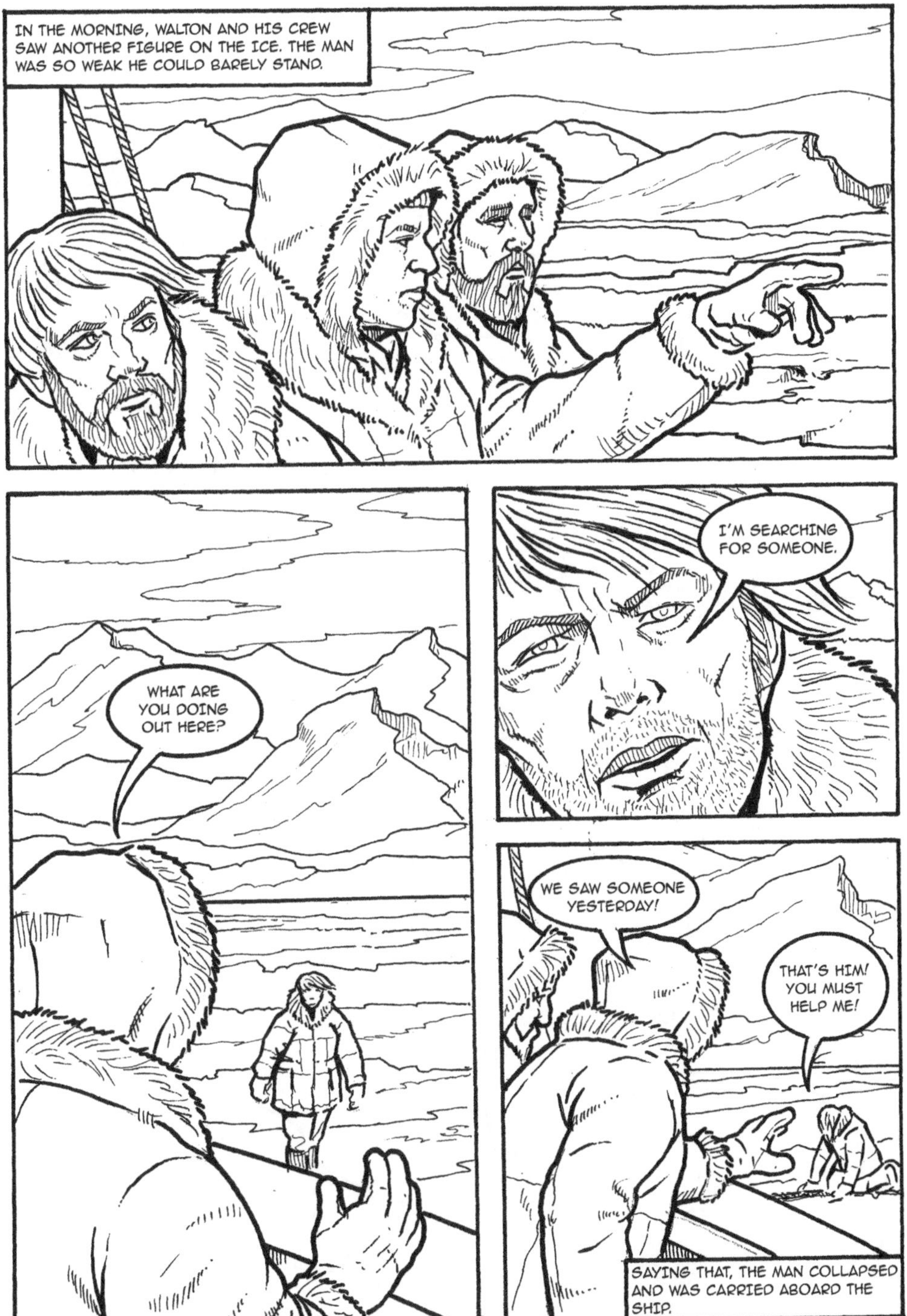
IN THE MORNING, WALTON AND HIS CREW SAW ANOTHER FIGURE ON THE ICE. THE MAN WAS SO WEAK HE COULD BARELY STAND.
WHAT ARE YOU DOING OUT HERE?
I'M SEARCHING FOR SOMEONE.
WE SAW SOMEONE YESTERDAY!
THAT'S HIM! YOU MUST HELP ME!
SAYING THAT, THE MAN COLLAPSED AND WAS CARRIED ABOARD THE SHIP.

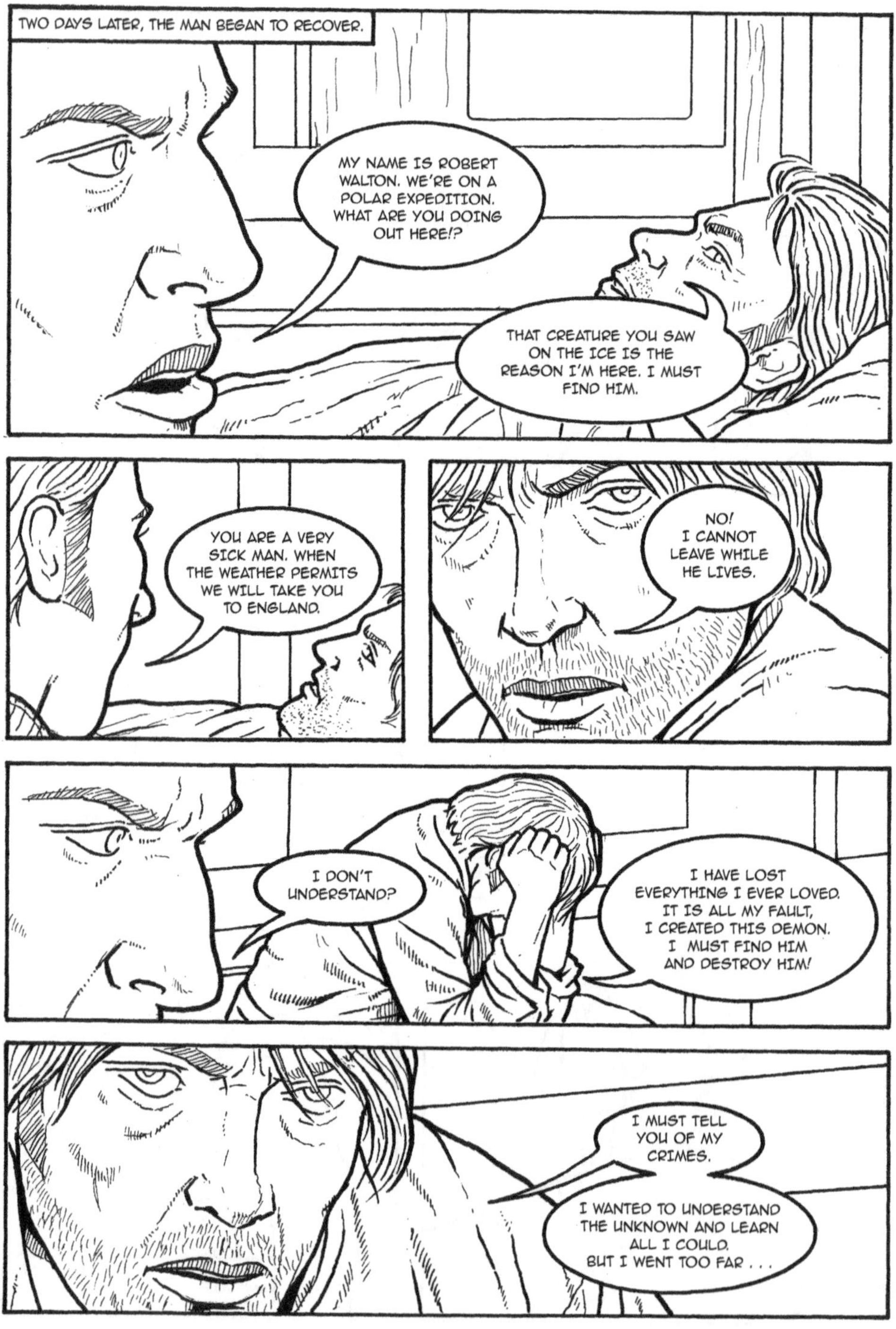
TWO DAYS LATER, THE MAN BEGAN TO RECOVER.
MY NAME IS ROBERT WALTON. WE'RE ON A POLAR EXPEDITION. WHAT ARE YOU DOING OUT HERE!?
THAT CREATURE YOU SAW ON THE ICE IS THE REASON I'M HERE. I MUST FIND HIM.
YOU ARE A VERY SICK MAN. WHEN THE WEATHER PERMITS WE WILL TAKE YOU TO ENGLAND.
NO! I CANNOT LEAVE WHILE HE LIVES.
I DON'T UNDERSTAND?
I HAVE LOST EVERYTHING I EVER LOVED. IT IS ALL MY FAULT, I CREATED THIS DEMON. I MUST FIND HIM AND DESTROY HIM!
I MUST TELL YOU OF MY CRIMES.
I WANTED TO UNDERSTAND THE UNKNOWN AND LEARN ALL I COULD. BUT I WENT TOO FAR . . .

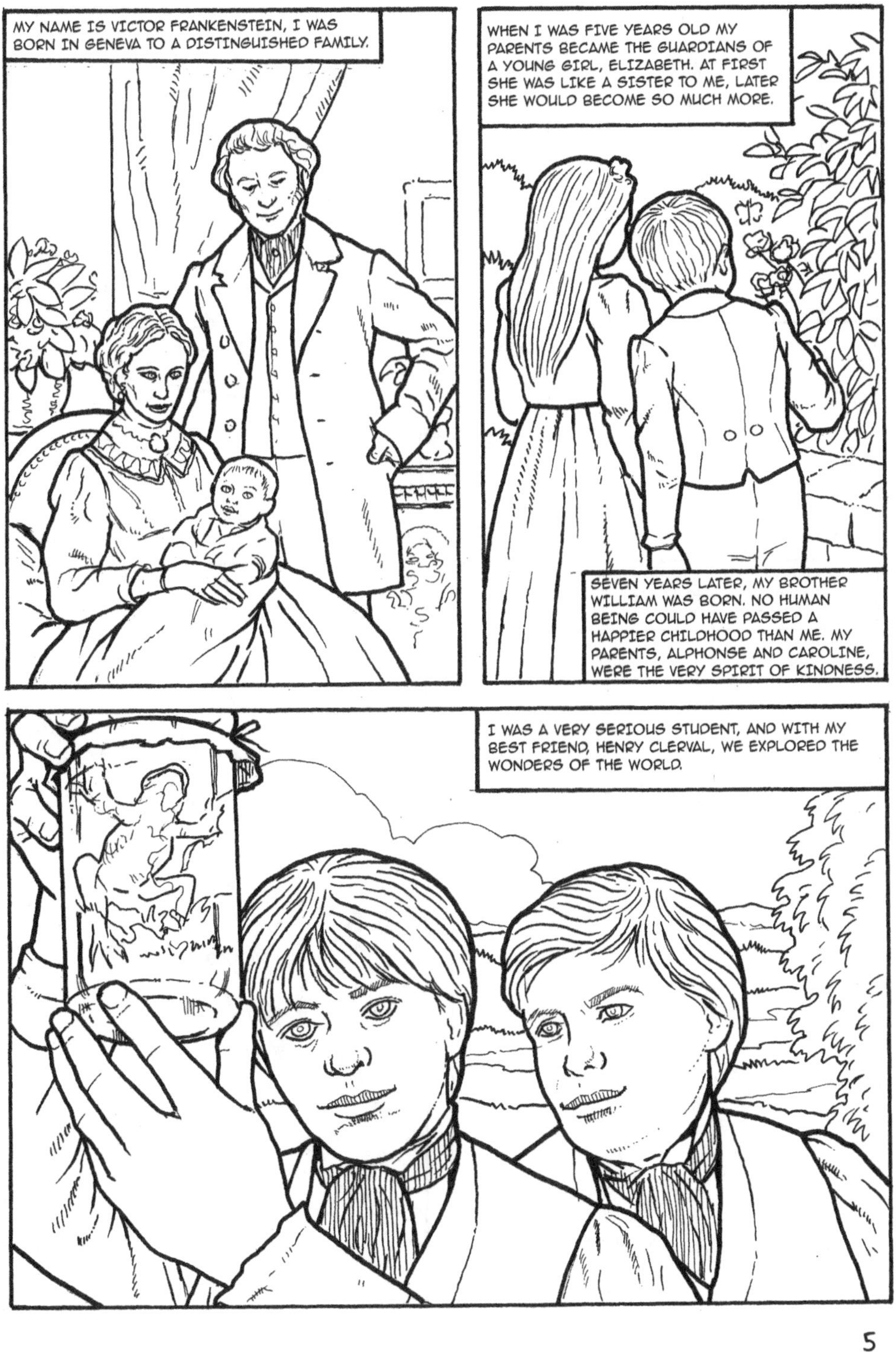
MY NAME IS VICTOR FRANKENSTEIN, I WAS BORN IN GENEVA TO A DISTINGUISHED FAMILY.
WHEN I WAS FIVE YEARS OLD MY PARENTS BECAME THE GUARDIANS OF A YOUNG GIRL, ELIZABETH. AT FIRST SHE WAS LIKE A SISTER TO ME, LATER SHE WOULD BECOME SO MUCH MORE.
SEVEN YEARS LATER, MY BROTHER WILLIAM WAS BORN. NO HUMAN BEING COULD HAVE PASSED A HAPPIER CHILDHOOD THAN ME. MY PARENTS, ALPHONSE AND CAROLINE, WERE THE VERY SPIRIT OF KINDNESS.
I WAS A VERY SERIOUS STUDENT, AND WITH MY BEST FRIEND, HENRY CLERVAL, WE EXPLORED THE WONDERS OF THE WORLD.

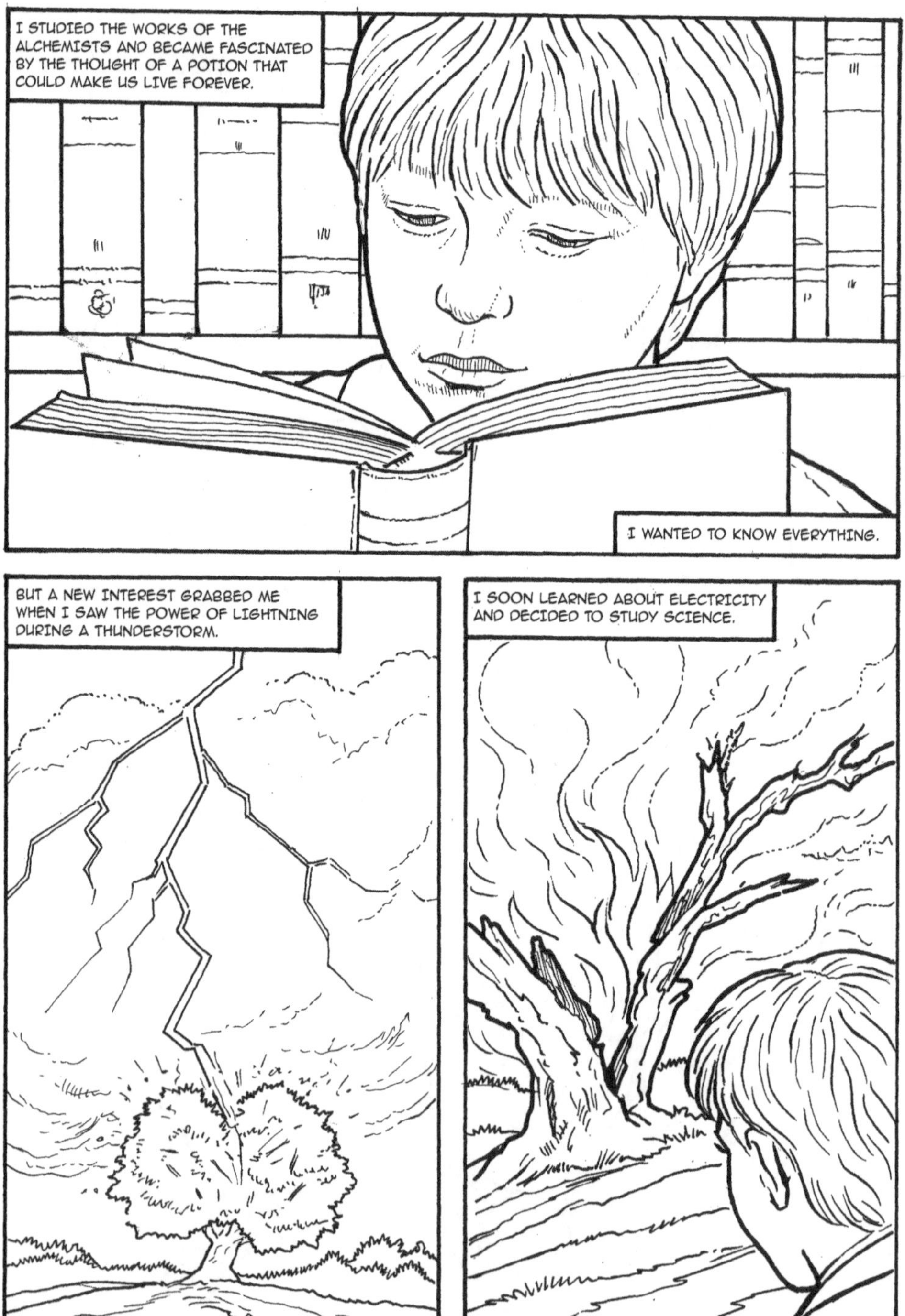
I STUDIED THE WORKS OF THE ALCHEMISTS AND BECAME FASCINATED BY THE THOUGHT OF A POTION THAT COULD MAKE US LIVE FOREVER.
I WANTED TO KNOW EVERYTHING.
BUT A NEW INTEREST GRABBED ME WHEN I SAW THE POWER OF LIGHTNING DURING A THUNDERSTORM.
I SOON LEARNED ABOUT ELECTRICITY AND DECIDED TO STUDY SCIENCE.

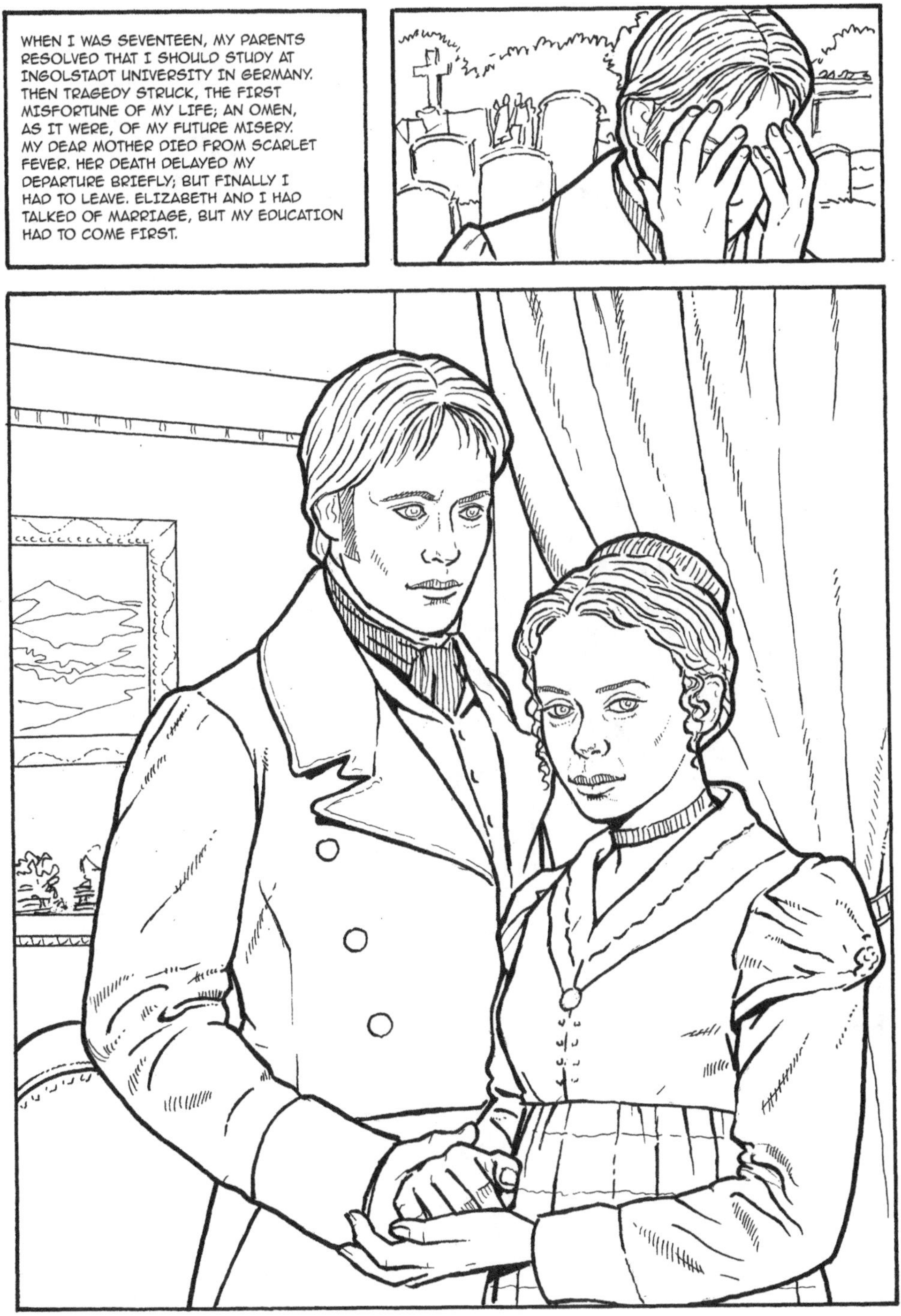
WHEN I WAS SEVENTEEN, MY PARENTS RESOLVED THAT I SHOULD STUDY AT INGOLSTADT UNIVERSITY IN GERMANY. THEN TRAGEDY STRUCK, THE FIRST MISFORTUNE OF MY LIFE; AN OMEN, AS IT WERE, OF MY FUTURE MISERY. MY DEAR MOTHER DIED FROM SCARLET FEVER. HER DEATH DELAYED MY DEPARTURE BRIEFLY; BUT FINALLY I HAD TO LEAVE. ELIZABETH AND I HAD TALKED OF MARRIAGE, BUT MY EDUCATION HAD TO COME FIRST.

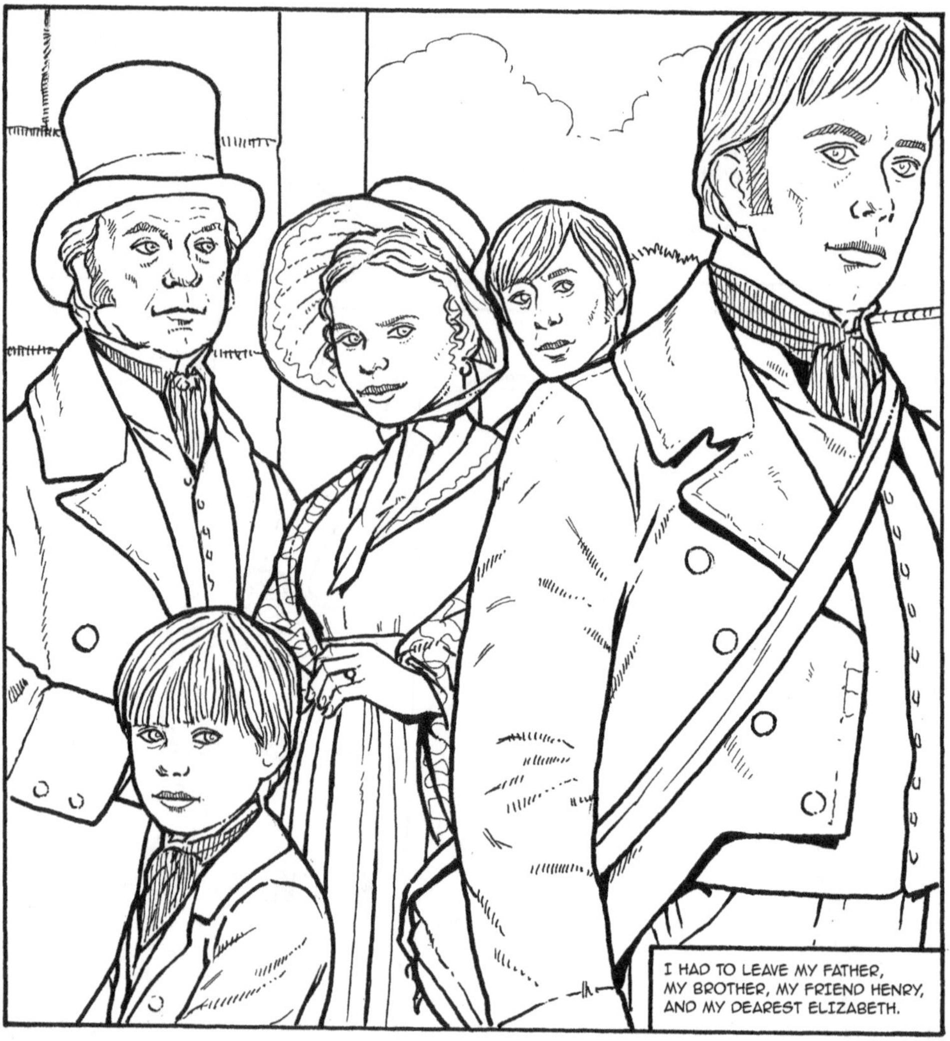
I HAD TO LEAVE MY FATHER,
MY BROTHER, MY FRIEND HENRY,
AND MY DEAREST ELIZABETH.

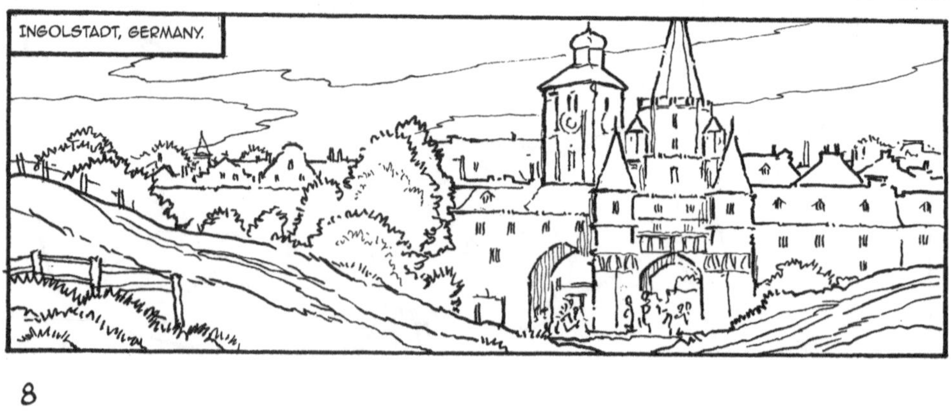
INGOLSTADT, GERMANY.

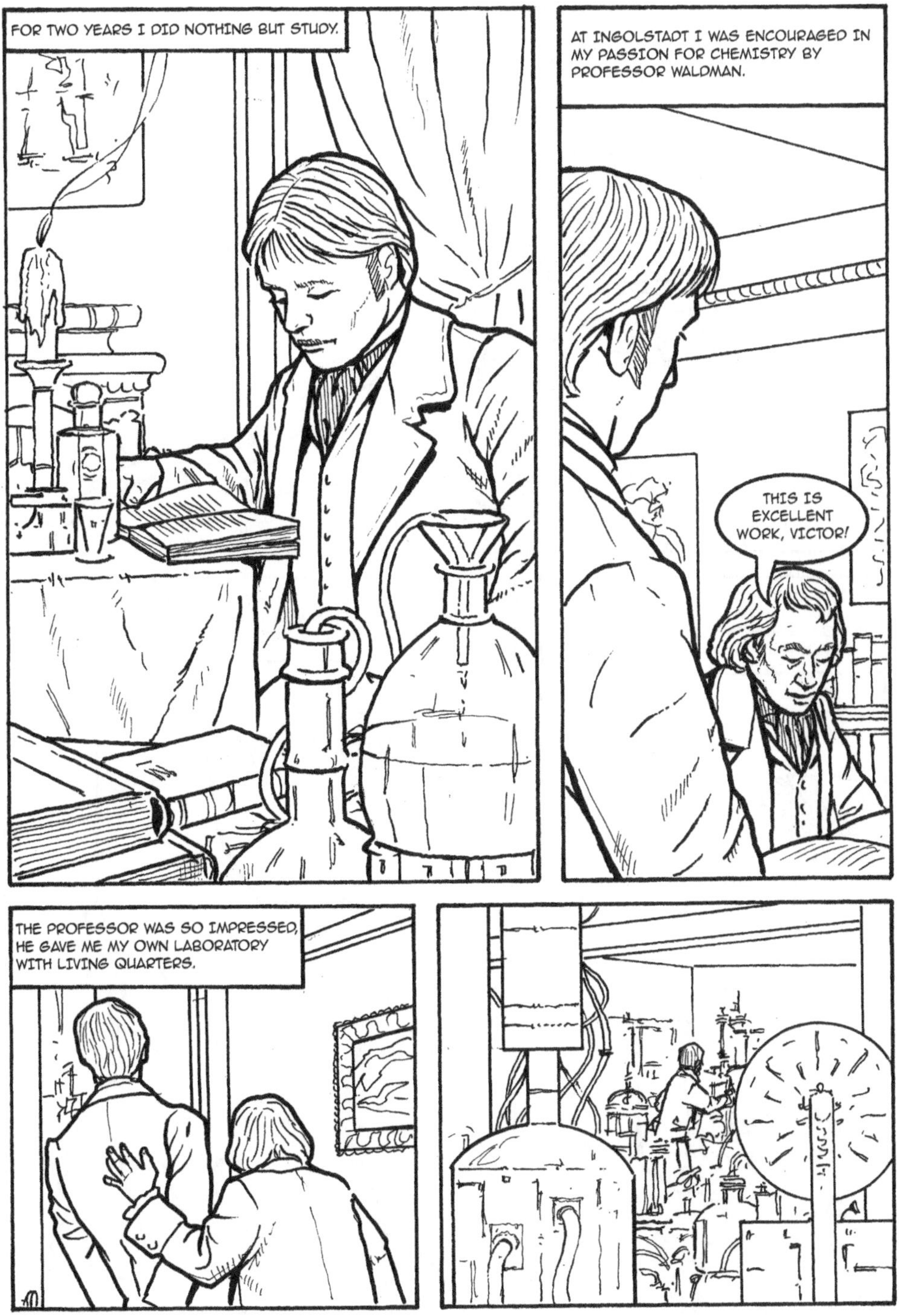
FOR TWO YEARS I DID NOTHING BUT STUDY.
AT INGOLSTADT I WAS ENCOURAGED IN MY PASSION FOR CHEMISTRY BY PROFESSOR WALDMAN.
THIS IS EXCELLENT WORK, VICTOR!
THE PROFESSOR WAS SO IMPRESSED, HE GAVE ME MY OWN LABORATORY WITH LIVING QUARTERS.

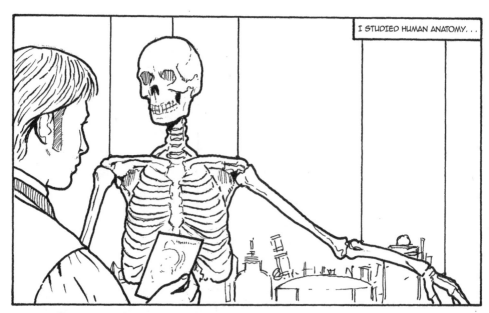

I STUDIED HUMAN ANATOMY. . .

. . . I STUDIED HOW LIFE WORKED AND WHAT CAUSED DEATH. I WAS LED TO EXAMINE THE CAUSE AND PROGRESS OF DECAY.

I SUCCEEDED IN DISCOVERING THE CAUSE OF GENERATION AND LIFE; INDEED, I BESTOWED ANIMATION UPON LIFELESS MATTER.

I BEGAN TO DEVELOP AN IDEA; I SHOULD ATTEMPT THE CREATION OF LIFE; A BEING LIKE MYSELF . . .

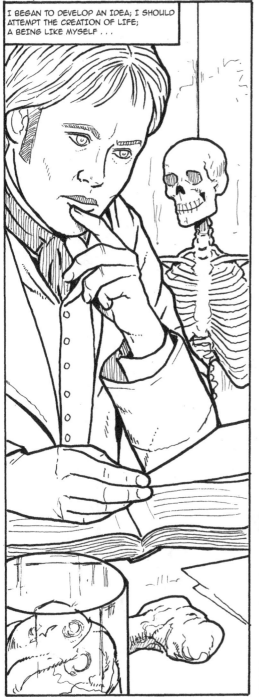

. . . A MAN, I WOULD CREATE A MAN!

I RESOLVED TO MAKE THE BEING OF A GIGANTIC STATURE, AT LEAST EIGHT FEET TALL . . .

. . . I RETURNED TO THE GRAVEYARD.

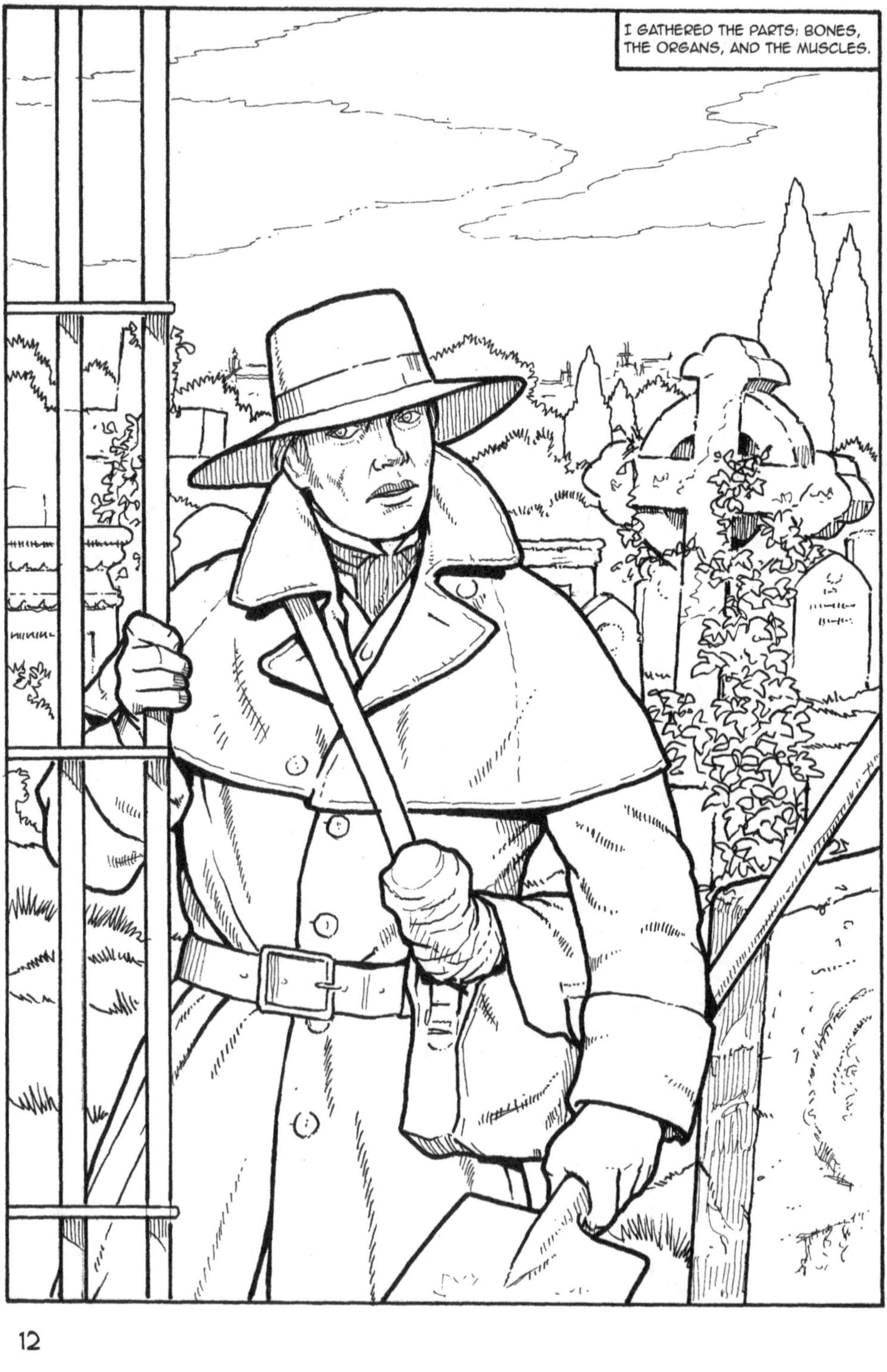
I GATHERED THE PARTS: BONES,
THE ORGANS, AND THE MUSCLES.

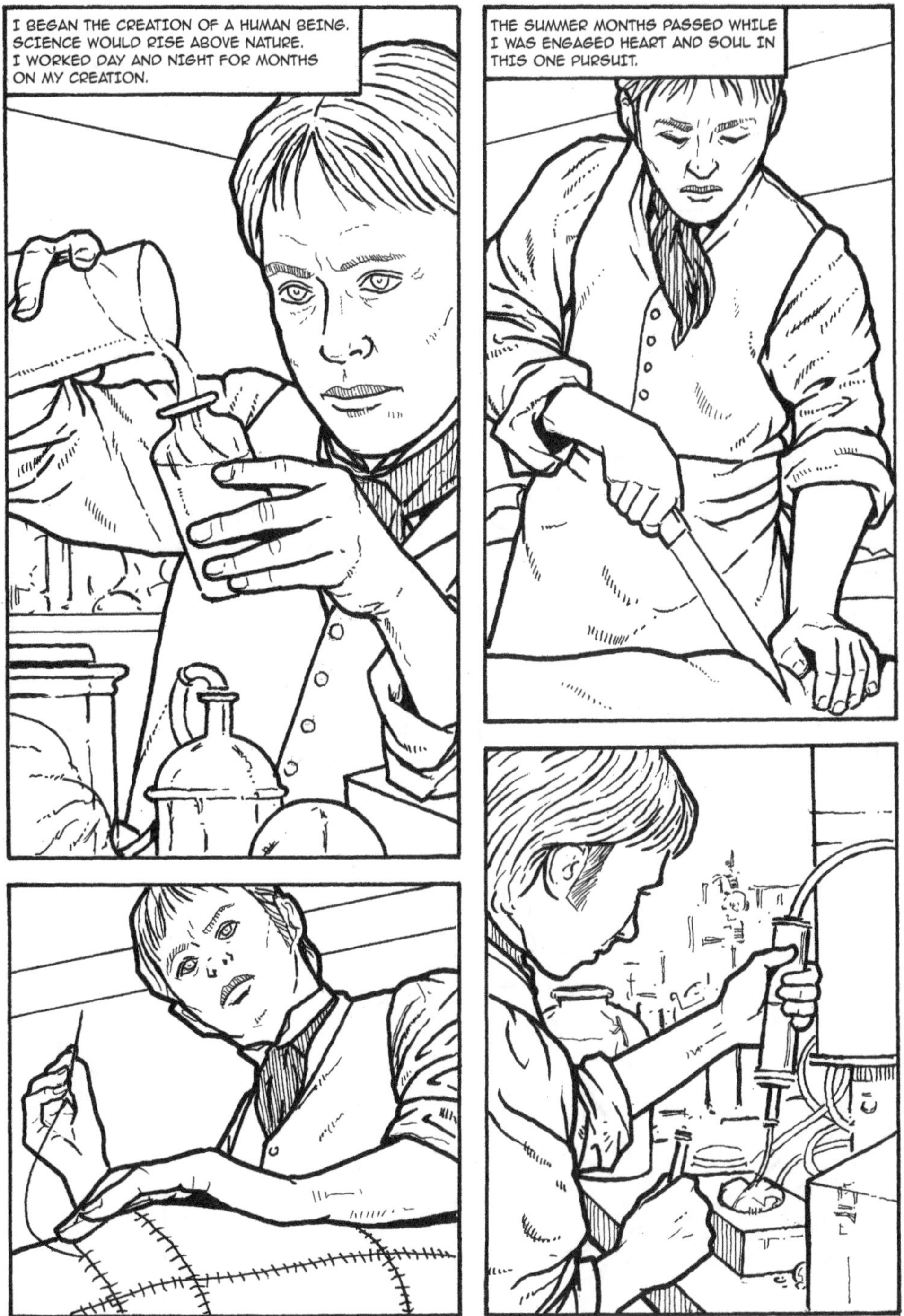

I BEGAN THE CREATION OF A HUMAN BEING. SCIENCE WOULD RISE ABOVE NATURE. I WORKED DAY AND NIGHT FOR MONTHS ON MY CREATION.
THE SUMMER MONTHS PASSED WHILE I WAS ENGAGED HEART AND SOUL IN THIS ONE PURSUIT.

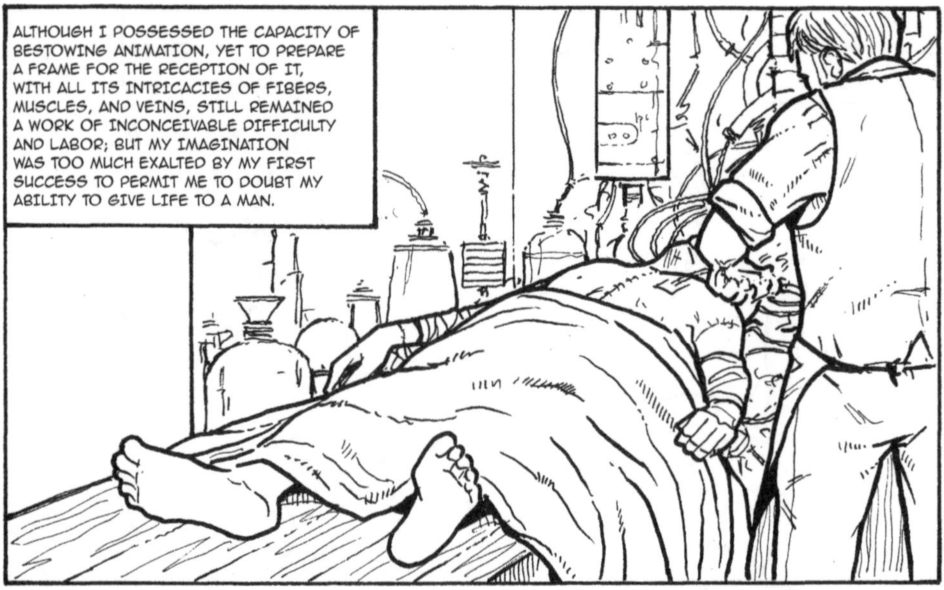
ALTHOUGH I POSSESSED THE CAPACITY OF BESTOWING ANIMATION, YET TO PREPARE A FRAME FOR THE RECEPTION OF IT, WITH ALL ITS INTRICACIES OF FIBERS, MUSCLES, AND VEINS, STILL REMAINED A WORK OF INCONCEIVABLE DIFFICULTY AND LABOR; BUT MY IMAGINATION WAS TOO MUCH EXALTED BY MY FIRST SUCCESS TO PERMIT ME TO DOUBT MY ABILITY TO GIVE LIFE TO A MAN.

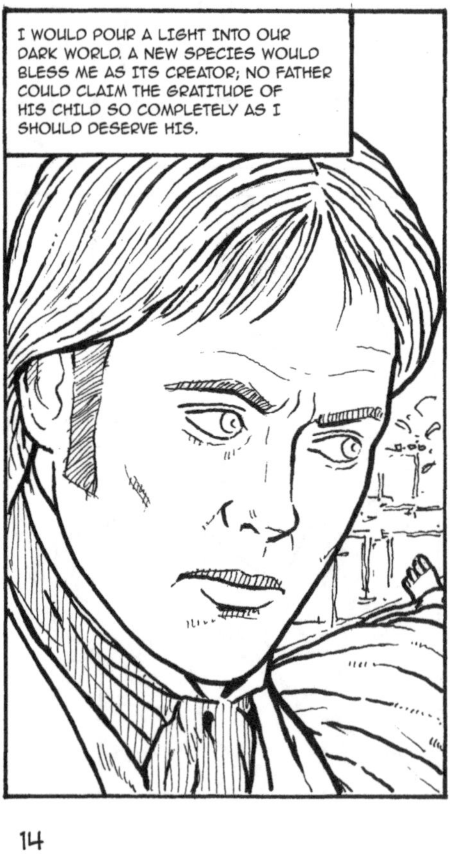
I WOULD POUR A LIGHT INTO OUR DARK WORLD. A NEW SPECIES WOULD BLESS ME AS ITS CREATOR; NO FATHER COULD CLAIM THE GRATITUDE OF HIS CHILD SO COMPLETELY AS I SHOULD DESERVE HIS.

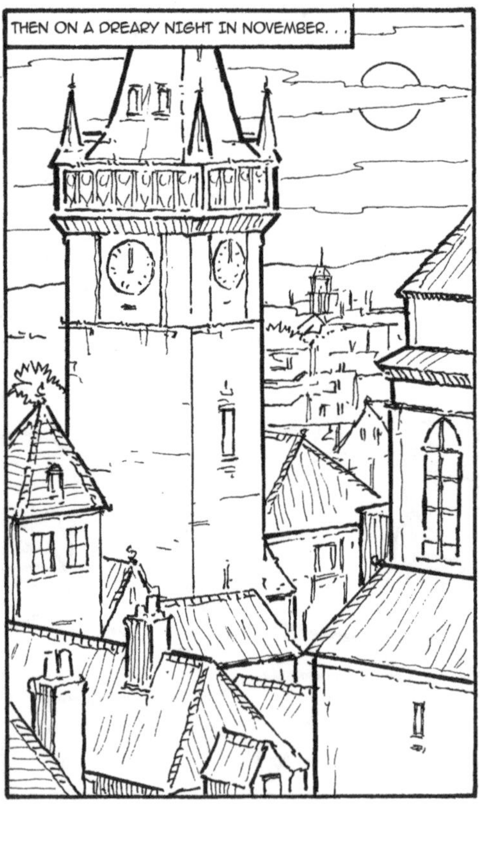
THEN ON A DREARY NIGHT IN NOVEMBER. . .

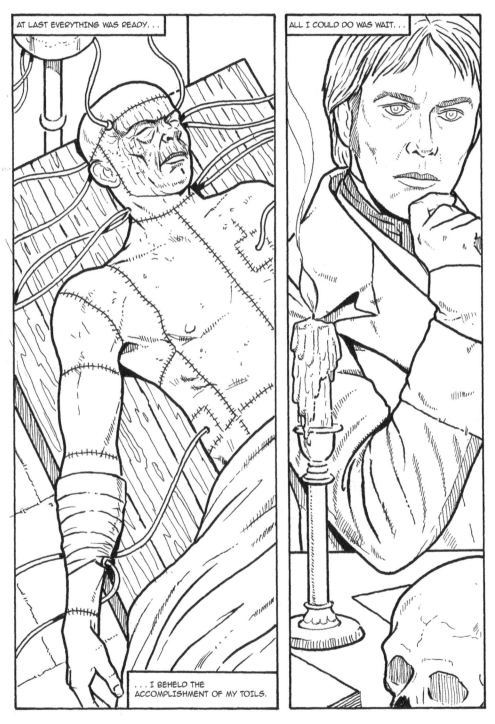

AT LAST EVERYTHING WAS READY...

ALL I COULD DO WAS WAIT...

...I BEHELD THE ACCOMPLISHMENT OF MY TOILS.

15

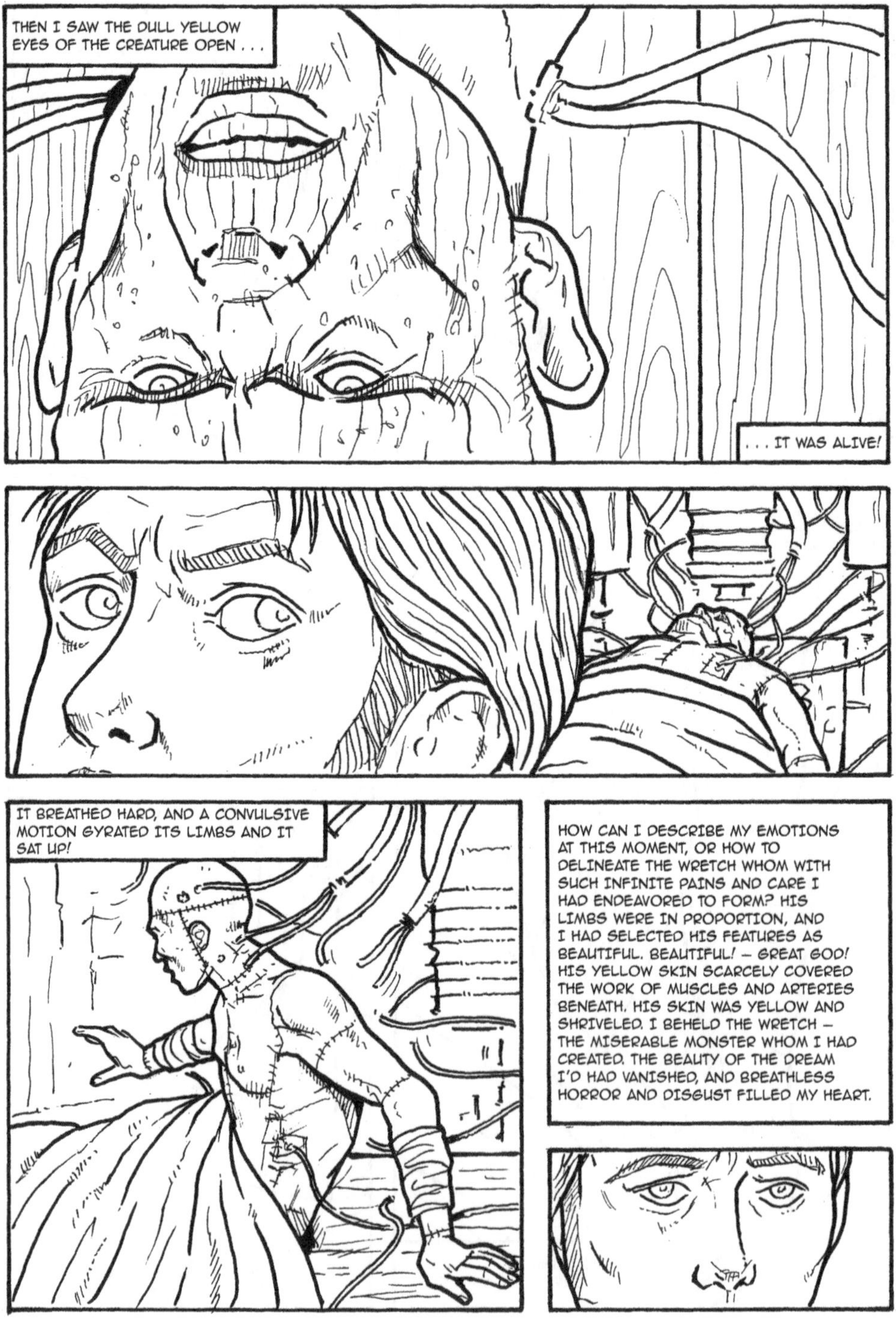
THEN I SAW THE DULL YELLOW EYES OF THE CREATURE OPEN . . .
. . . IT WAS ALIVE!
IT BREATHED HARD, AND A CONVULSIVE MOTION GYRATED ITS LIMBS AND IT SAT UP!
HOW CAN I DESCRIBE MY EMOTIONS AT THIS MOMENT, OR HOW TO DELINEATE THE WRETCH WHOM WITH SUCH INFINITE PAINS AND CARE I HAD ENDEAVORED TO FORM? HIS LIMBS WERE IN PROPORTION, AND I HAD SELECTED HIS FEATURES AS BEAUTIFUL. BEAUTIFUL! – GREAT GOD! HIS YELLOW SKIN SCARCELY COVERED THE WORK OF MUSCLES AND ARTERIES BENEATH. HIS SKIN WAS YELLOW AND SHRIVELED. I BEHELD THE WRETCH – THE MISERABLE MONSTER WHOM I HAD CREATED. THE BEAUTY OF THE DREAM I'D HAD VANISHED, AND BREATHLESS HORROR AND DISGUST FILLED MY HEART.

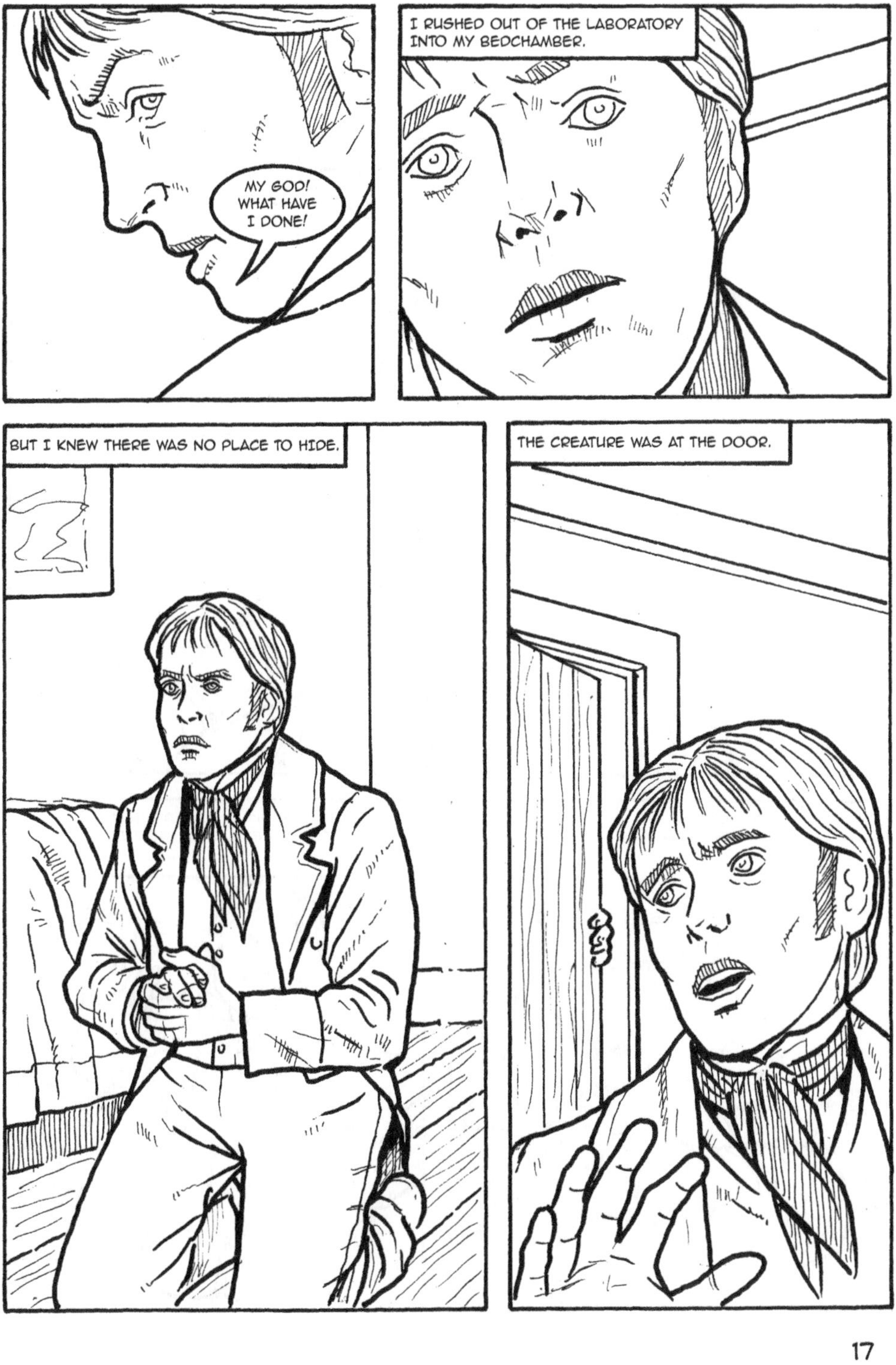
MY GOD! WHAT HAVE I DONE!
I RUSHED OUT OF THE LABORATORY INTO MY BEDCHAMBER.
BUT I KNEW THERE WAS NO PLACE TO HIDE.
THE CREATURE WAS AT THE DOOR.

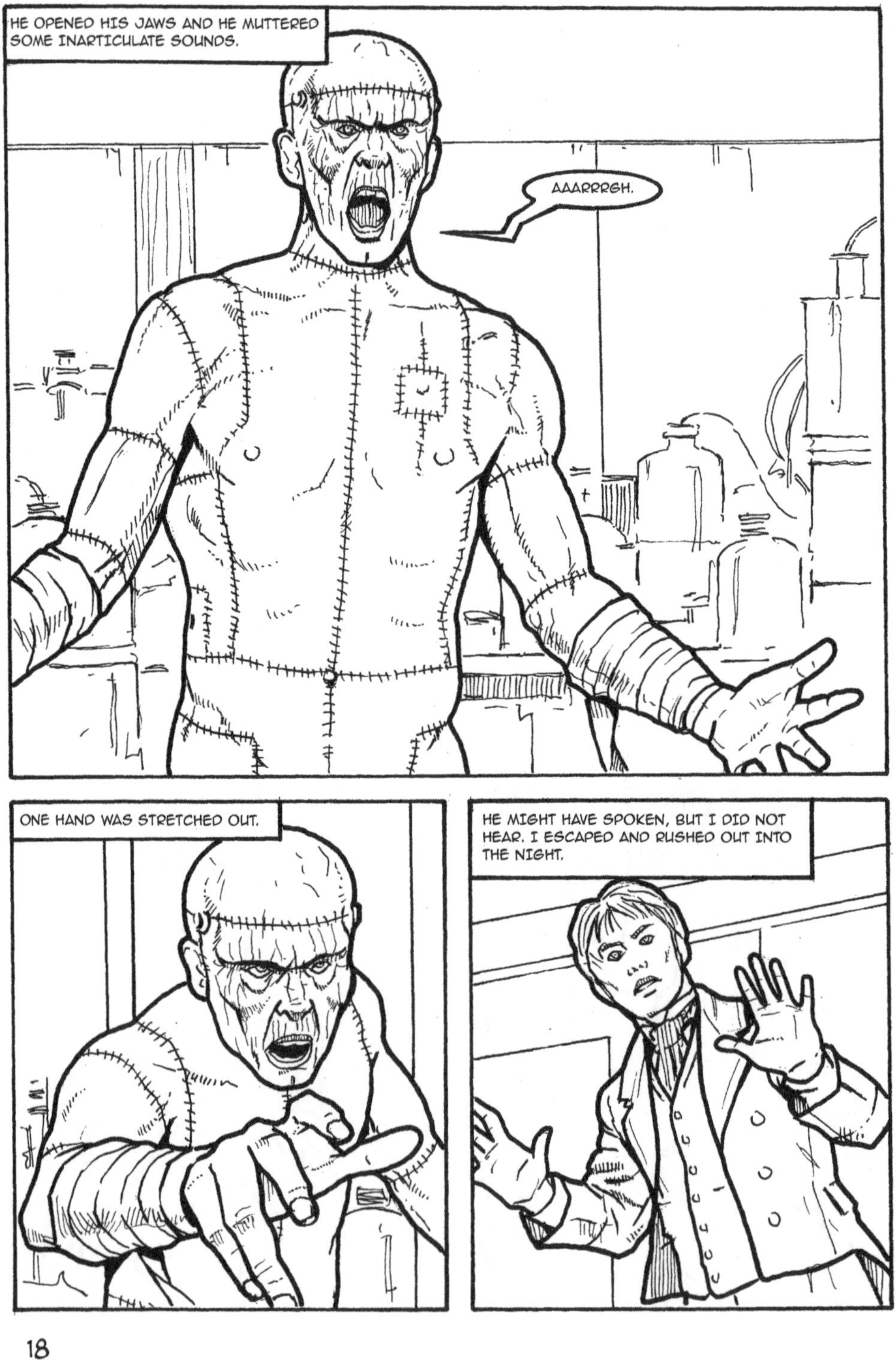
HE OPENED HIS JAWS AND HE MUTTERED SOME INARTICULATE SOUNDS.
AAARRRGH.
ONE HAND WAS STRETCHED OUT.
HE MIGHT HAVE SPOKEN, BUT I DID NOT HEAR. I ESCAPED AND RUSHED OUT INTO THE NIGHT.

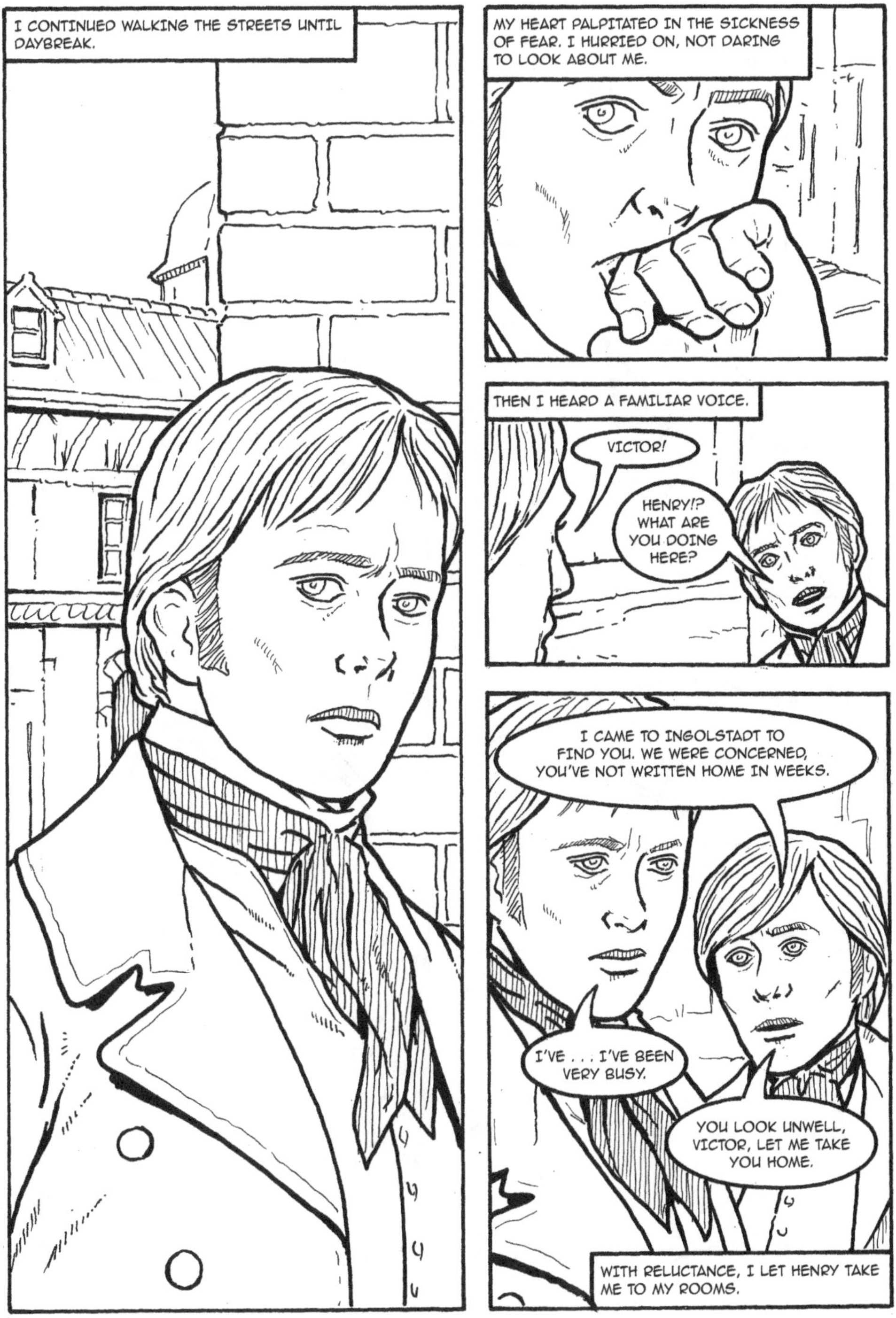
I CONTINUED WALKING THE STREETS UNTIL DAYBREAK.
MY HEART PALPITATED IN THE SICKNESS OF FEAR. I HURRIED ON, NOT DARING TO LOOK ABOUT ME.
THEN I HEARD A FAMILIAR VOICE.
VICTOR!
HENRY!? WHAT ARE YOU DOING HERE?
I CAME TO INGOLSTADT TO FIND YOU. WE WERE CONCERNED, YOU'VE NOT WRITTEN HOME IN WEEKS.
I'VE . . . I'VE BEEN VERY BUSY.
YOU LOOK UNWELL, VICTOR, LET ME TAKE YOU HOME.
WITH RELUCTANCE, I LET HENRY TAKE ME TO MY ROOMS.

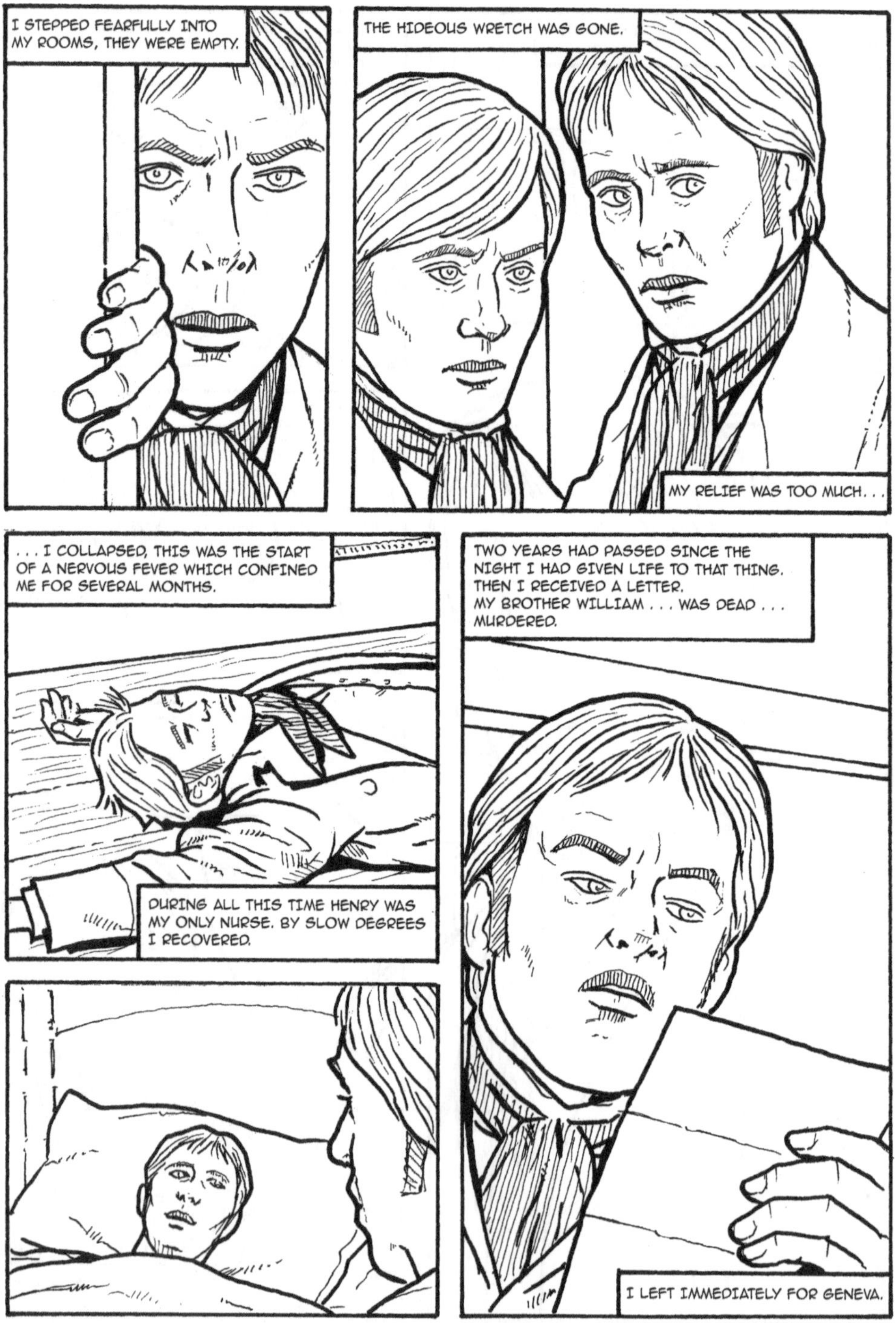
I STEPPED FEARFULLY INTO MY ROOMS, THEY WERE EMPTY.
THE HIDEOUS WRETCH WAS GONE.
MY RELIEF WAS TOO MUCH . . .
. . . I COLLAPSED, THIS WAS THE START OF A NERVOUS FEVER WHICH CONFINED ME FOR SEVERAL MONTHS.
DURING ALL THIS TIME HENRY WAS MY ONLY NURSE. BY SLOW DEGREES I RECOVERED.
TWO YEARS HAD PASSED SINCE THE NIGHT I HAD GIVEN LIFE TO THAT THING. THEN I RECEIVED A LETTER. MY BROTHER WILLIAM . . . WAS DEAD . . . MURDERED.
I LEFT IMMEDIATELY FOR GENEVA.

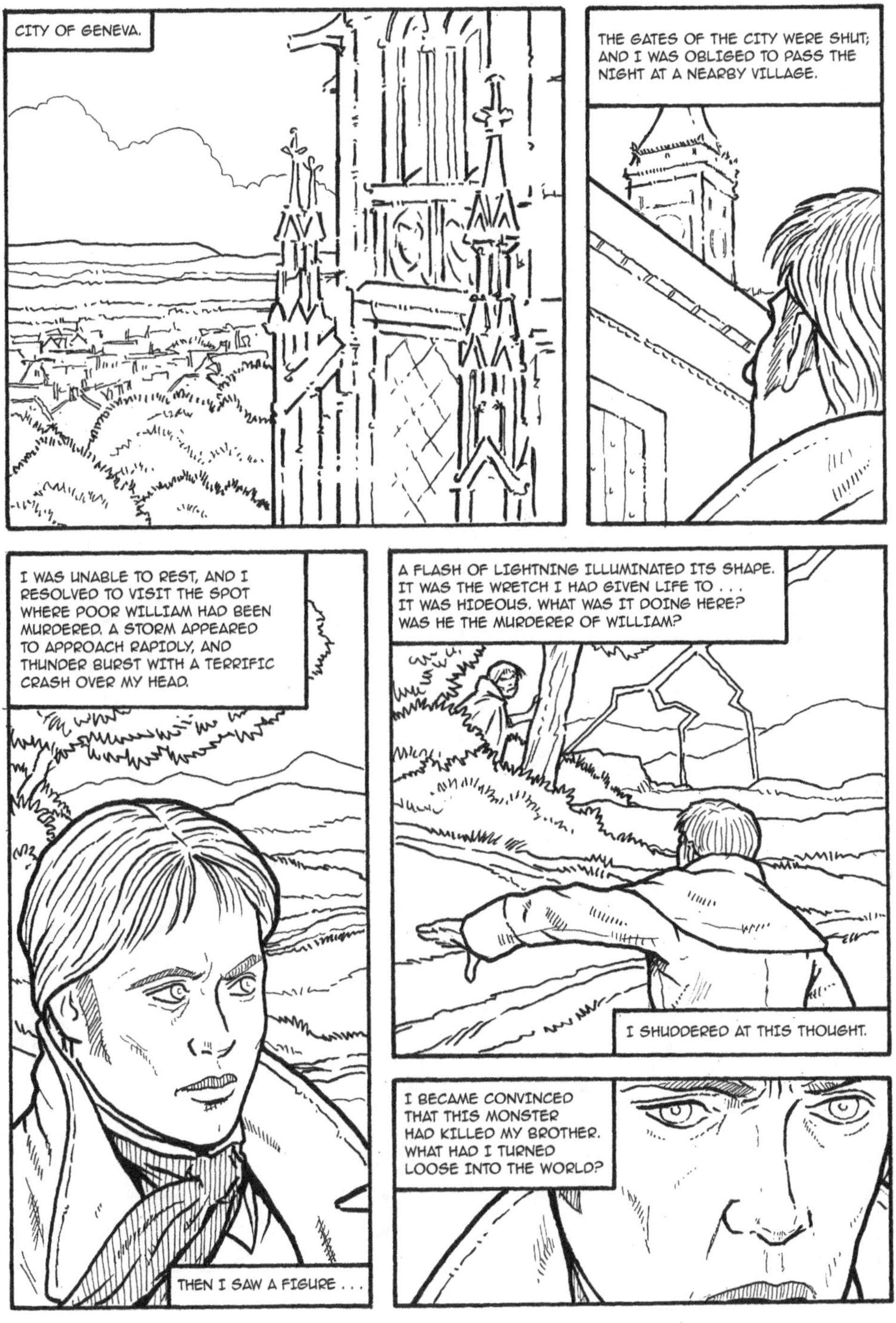
CITY OF GENEVA.
THE GATES OF THE CITY WERE SHUT; AND I WAS OBLIGED TO PASS THE NIGHT AT A NEARBY VILLAGE.
I WAS UNABLE TO REST, AND I RESOLVED TO VISIT THE SPOT WHERE POOR WILLIAM HAD BEEN MURDERED. A STORM APPEARED TO APPROACH RAPIDLY, AND THUNDER BURST WITH A TERRIFIC CRASH OVER MY HEAD.
THEN I SAW A FIGURE . . .
A FLASH OF LIGHTNING ILLUMINATED ITS SHAPE. IT WAS THE WRETCH I HAD GIVEN LIFE TO . . . IT WAS HIDEOUS. WHAT WAS IT DOING HERE? WAS HE THE MURDERER OF WILLIAM?
I SHUDDERED AT THIS THOUGHT.
I BECAME CONVINCED THAT THIS MONSTER HAD KILLED MY BROTHER. WHAT HAD I TURNED LOOSE INTO THE WORLD?

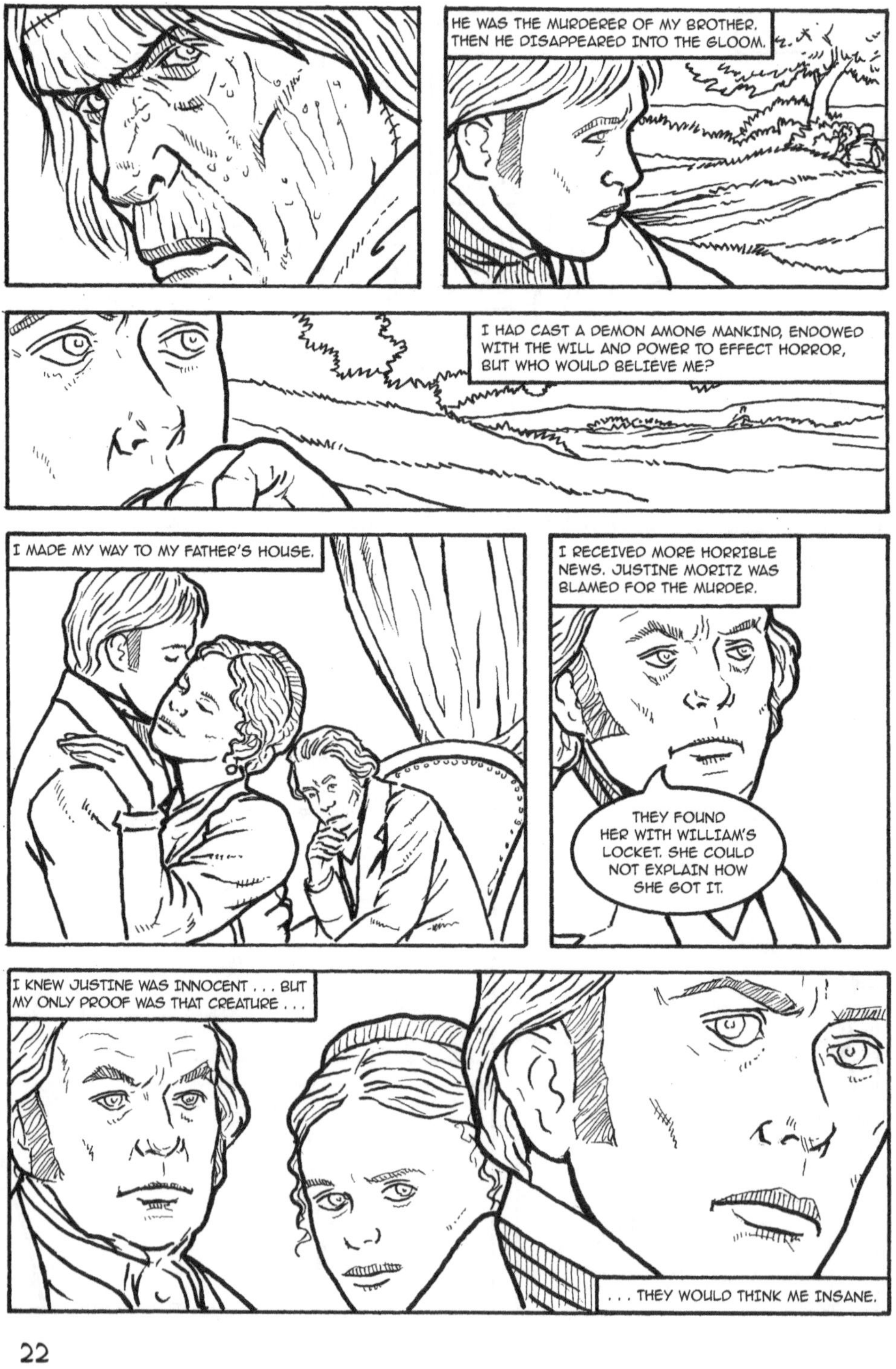
HE WAS THE MURDERER OF MY BROTHER. THEN HE DISAPPEARED INTO THE GLOOM.
I HAD CAST A DEMON AMONG MANKIND, ENDOWED WITH THE WILL AND POWER TO EFFECT HORROR, BUT WHO WOULD BELIEVE ME?
I MADE MY WAY TO MY FATHER'S HOUSE.
I RECEIVED MORE HORRIBLE NEWS. JUSTINE MORITZ WAS BLAMED FOR THE MURDER.
THEY FOUND HER WITH WILLIAM'S LOCKET. SHE COULD NOT EXPLAIN HOW SHE GOT IT.
I KNEW JUSTINE WAS INNOCENT . . . BUT MY ONLY PROOF WAS THAT CREATURE . . .
. . . THEY WOULD THINK ME INSANE.

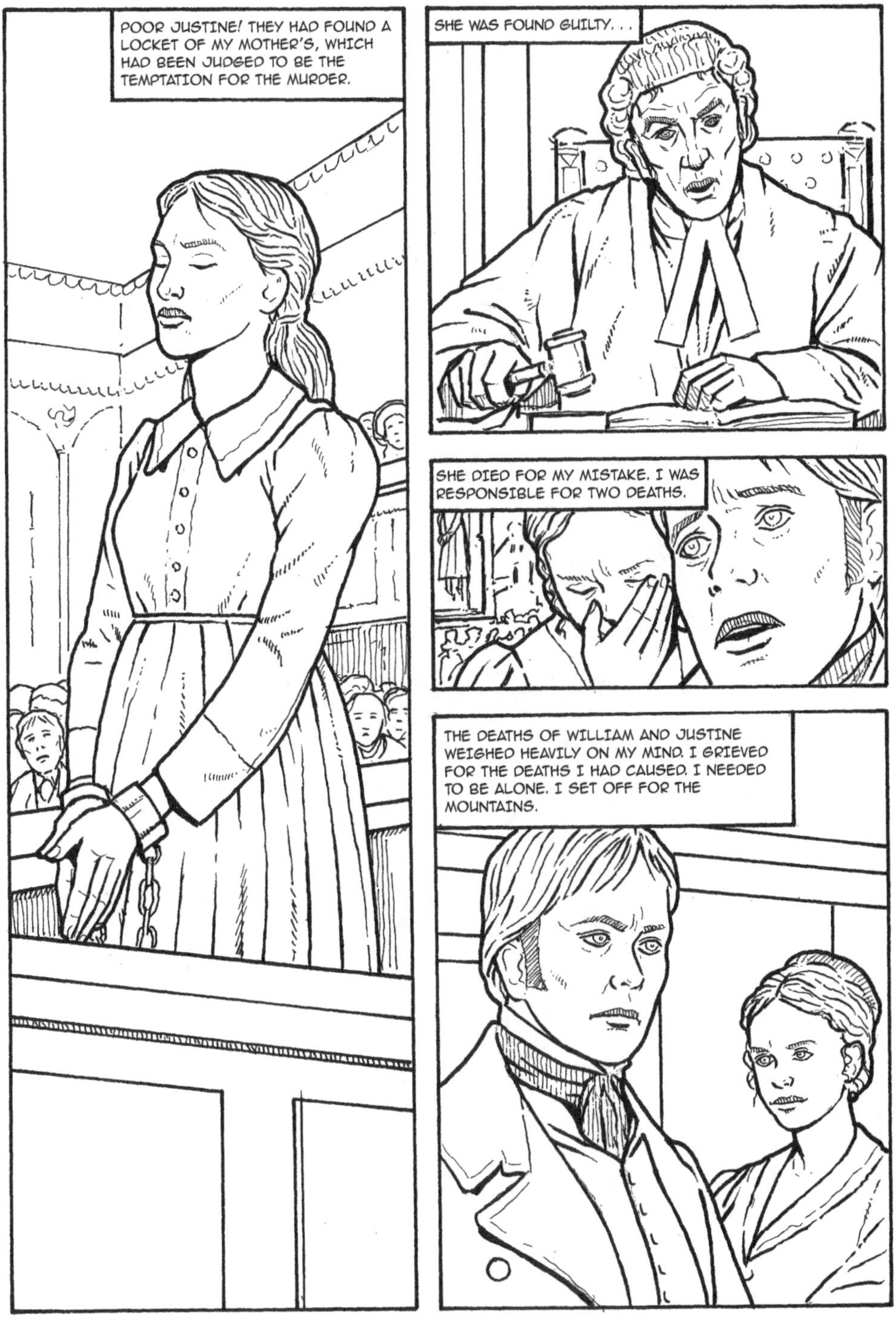
POOR JUSTINE! THEY HAD FOUND A LOCKET OF MY MOTHER'S, WHICH HAD BEEN JUDGED TO BE THE TEMPTATION FOR THE MURDER.
SHE WAS FOUND GUILTY. . .
SHE DIED FOR MY MISTAKE. I WAS RESPONSIBLE FOR TWO DEATHS.
THE DEATHS OF WILLIAM AND JUSTINE WEIGHED HEAVILY ON MY MIND. I GRIEVED FOR THE DEATHS I HAD CAUSED. I NEEDED TO BE ALONE. I SET OFF FOR THE MOUNTAINS.

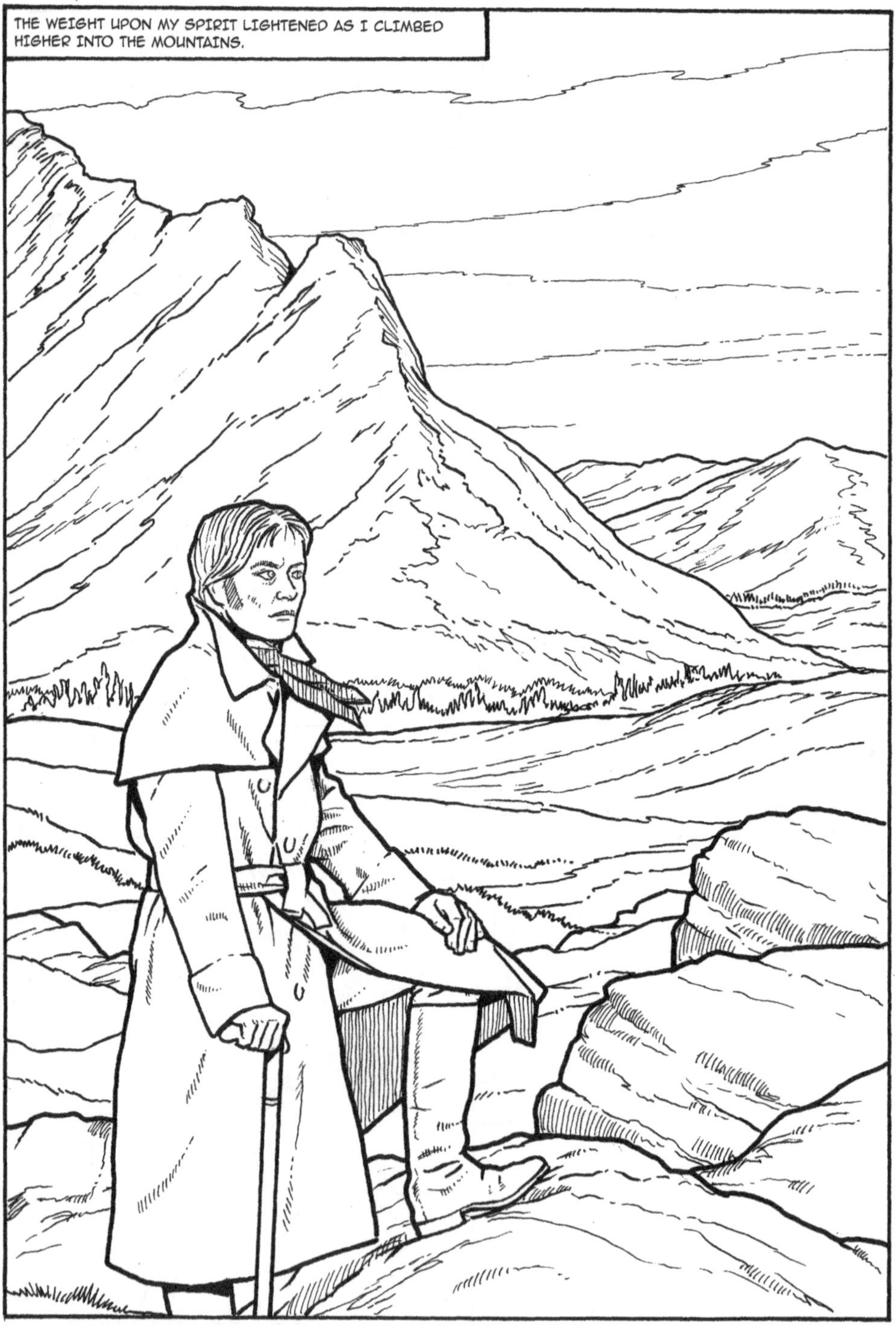
THE WEIGHT UPON MY SPIRIT LIGHTENED AS I CLIMBED HIGHER INTO THE MOUNTAINS.

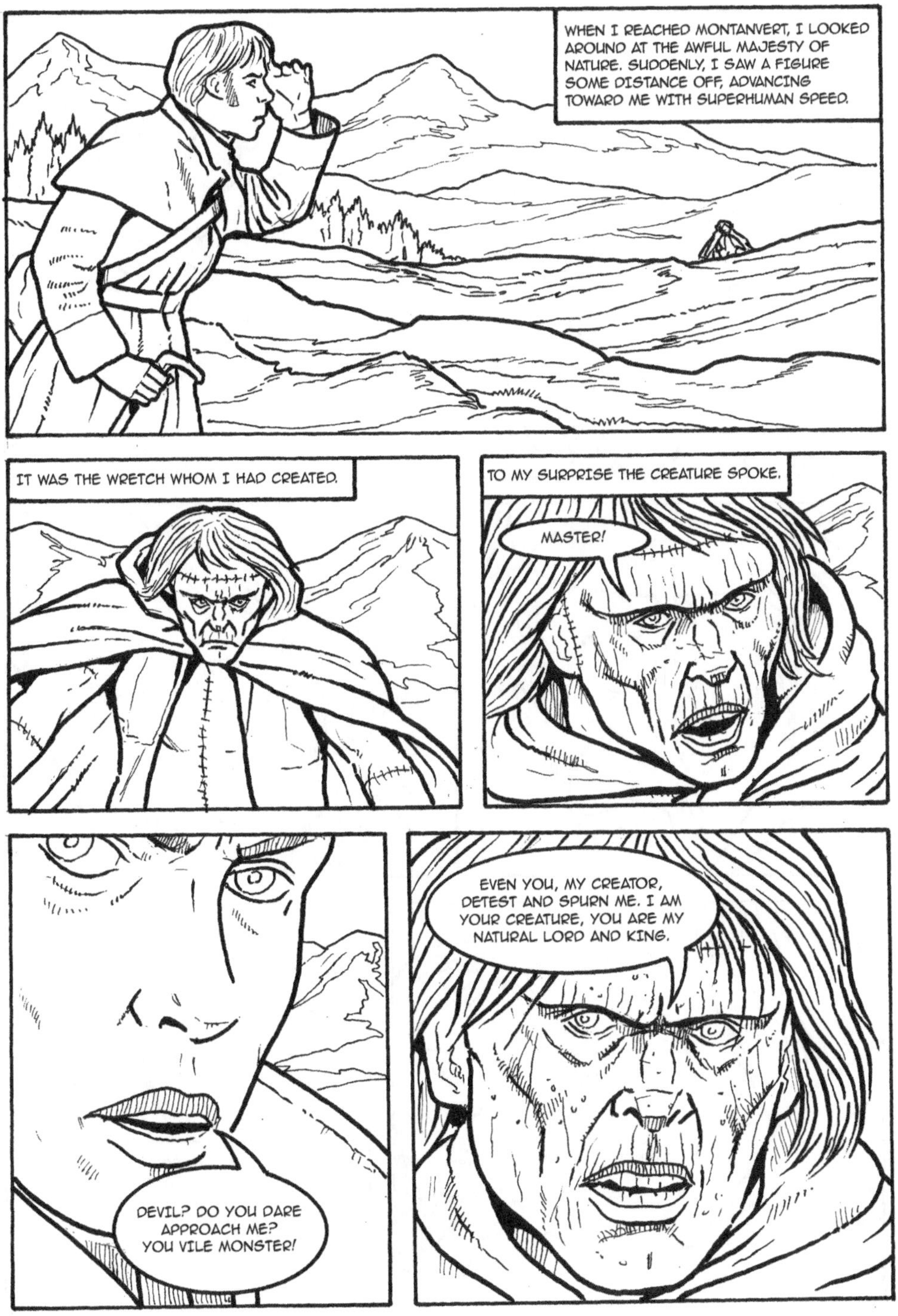
WHEN I REACHED MONTANVERT, I LOOKED AROUND AT THE AWFUL MAJESTY OF NATURE. SUDDENLY, I SAW A FIGURE SOME DISTANCE OFF, ADVANCING TOWARD ME WITH SUPERHUMAN SPEED.
IT WAS THE WRETCH WHOM I HAD CREATED.
TO MY SURPRISE THE CREATURE SPOKE.
MASTER!
DEVIL? DO YOU DARE APPROACH ME? YOU VILE MONSTER!
EVEN YOU, MY CREATOR, DETEST AND SPURN ME. I AM YOUR CREATURE, YOU ARE MY NATURAL LORD AND KING.

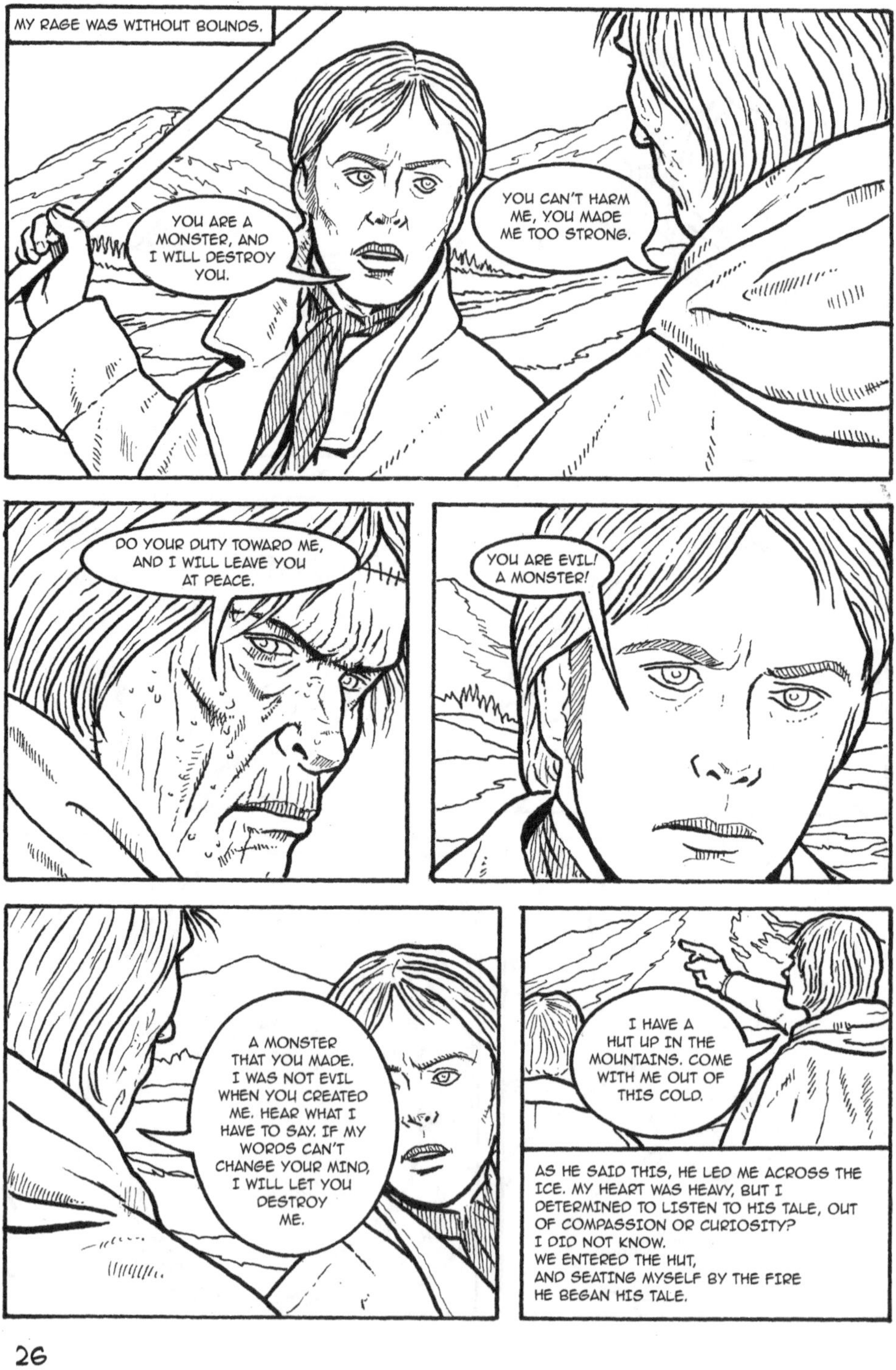
MY RAGE WAS WITHOUT BOUNDS.
YOU ARE A MONSTER, AND I WILL DESTROY YOU.
YOU CAN'T HARM ME, YOU MADE ME TOO STRONG.
DO YOUR DUTY TOWARD ME, AND I WILL LEAVE YOU AT PEACE.
YOU ARE EVIL! A MONSTER!
A MONSTER THAT YOU MADE. I WAS NOT EVIL WHEN YOU CREATED ME. HEAR WHAT I HAVE TO SAY. IF MY WORDS CAN'T CHANGE YOUR MIND, I WILL LET YOU DESTROY ME.
I HAVE A HUT UP IN THE MOUNTAINS. COME WITH ME OUT OF THIS COLD.
AS HE SAID THIS, HE LED ME ACROSS THE ICE. MY HEART WAS HEAVY, BUT I DETERMINED TO LISTEN TO HIS TALE, OUT OF COMPASSION OR CURIOSITY? I DID NOT KNOW. WE ENTERED THE HUT, AND SEATING MYSELF BY THE FIRE HE BEGAN HIS TALE.

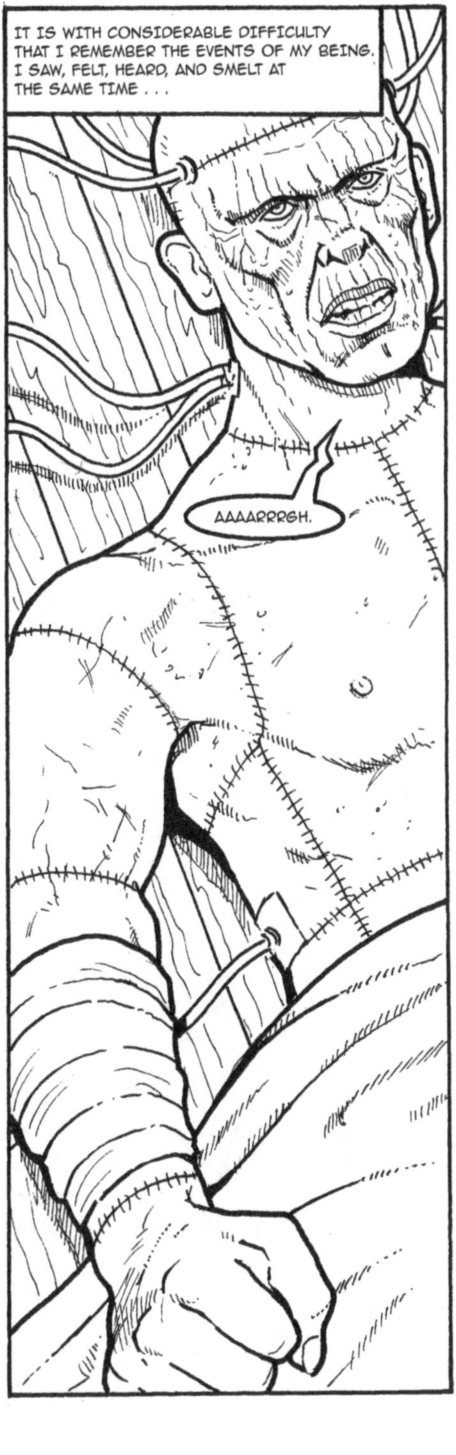
IT IS WITH CONSIDERABLE DIFFICULTY THAT I REMEMBER THE EVENTS OF MY BEING. I SAW, FELT, HEARD, AND SMELT AT THE SAME TIME . . .
AAAARRRGH.

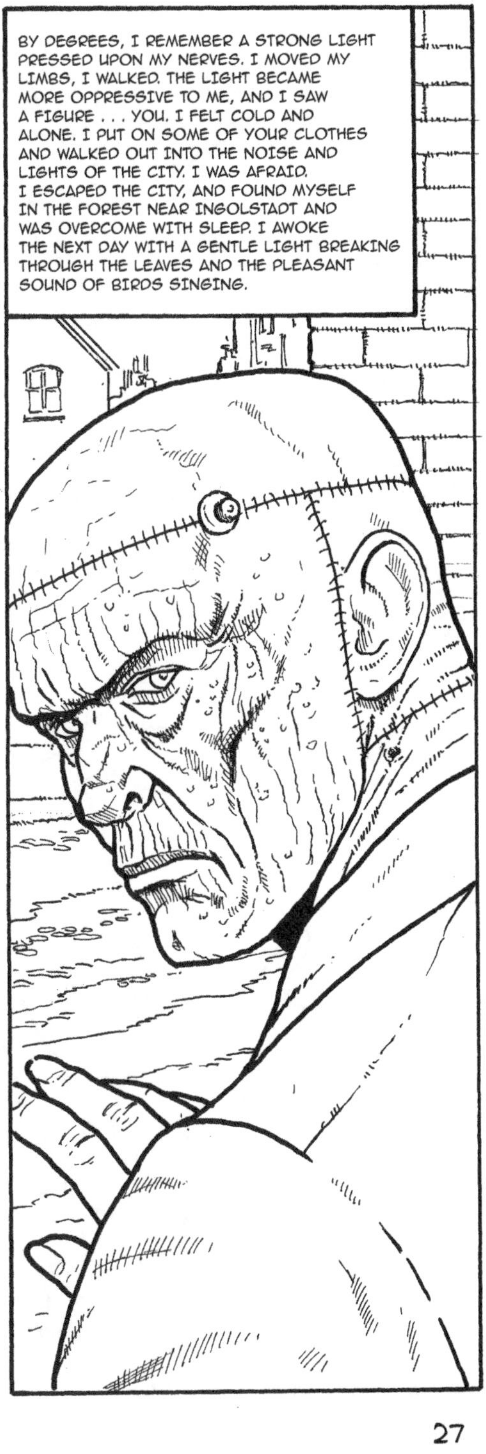
BY DEGREES, I REMEMBER A STRONG LIGHT PRESSED UPON MY NERVES. I MOVED MY LIMBS, I WALKED. THE LIGHT BECAME MORE OPPRESSIVE TO ME, AND I SAW A FIGURE . . . YOU. I FELT COLD AND ALONE. I PUT ON SOME OF YOUR CLOTHES AND WALKED OUT INTO THE NOISE AND LIGHTS OF THE CITY. I WAS AFRAID. I ESCAPED THE CITY, AND FOUND MYSELF IN THE FOREST NEAR INGOLSTADT AND WAS OVERCOME WITH SLEEP. I AWOKE THE NEXT DAY WITH A GENTLE LIGHT BREAKING THROUGH THE LEAVES AND THE PLEASANT SOUND OF BIRDS SINGING.

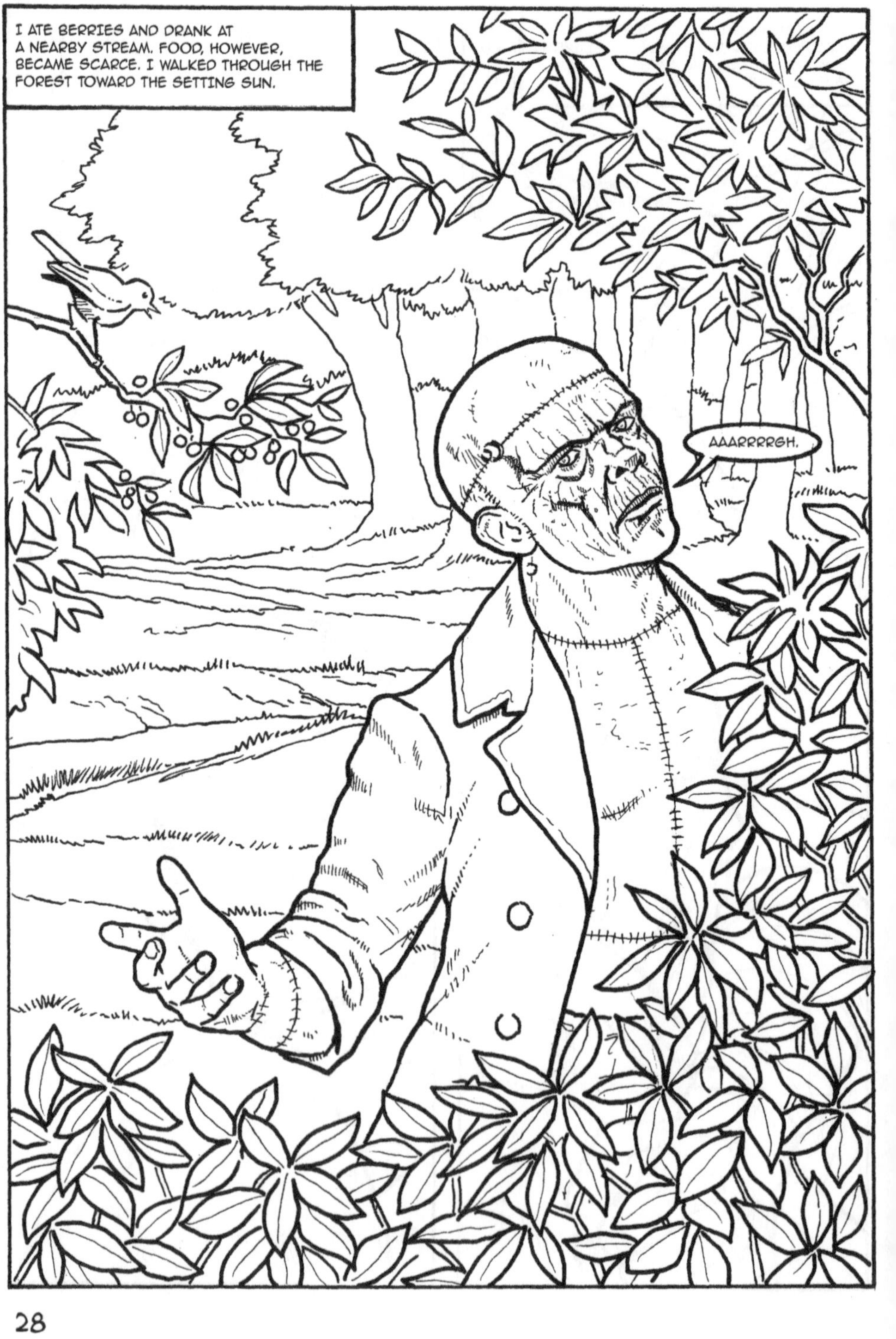
I ATE BERRIES AND DRANK AT A NEARBY STREAM. FOOD, HOWEVER, BECAME SCARCE. I WALKED THROUGH THE FOREST TOWARD THE SETTING SUN.
AAARRRRGH.

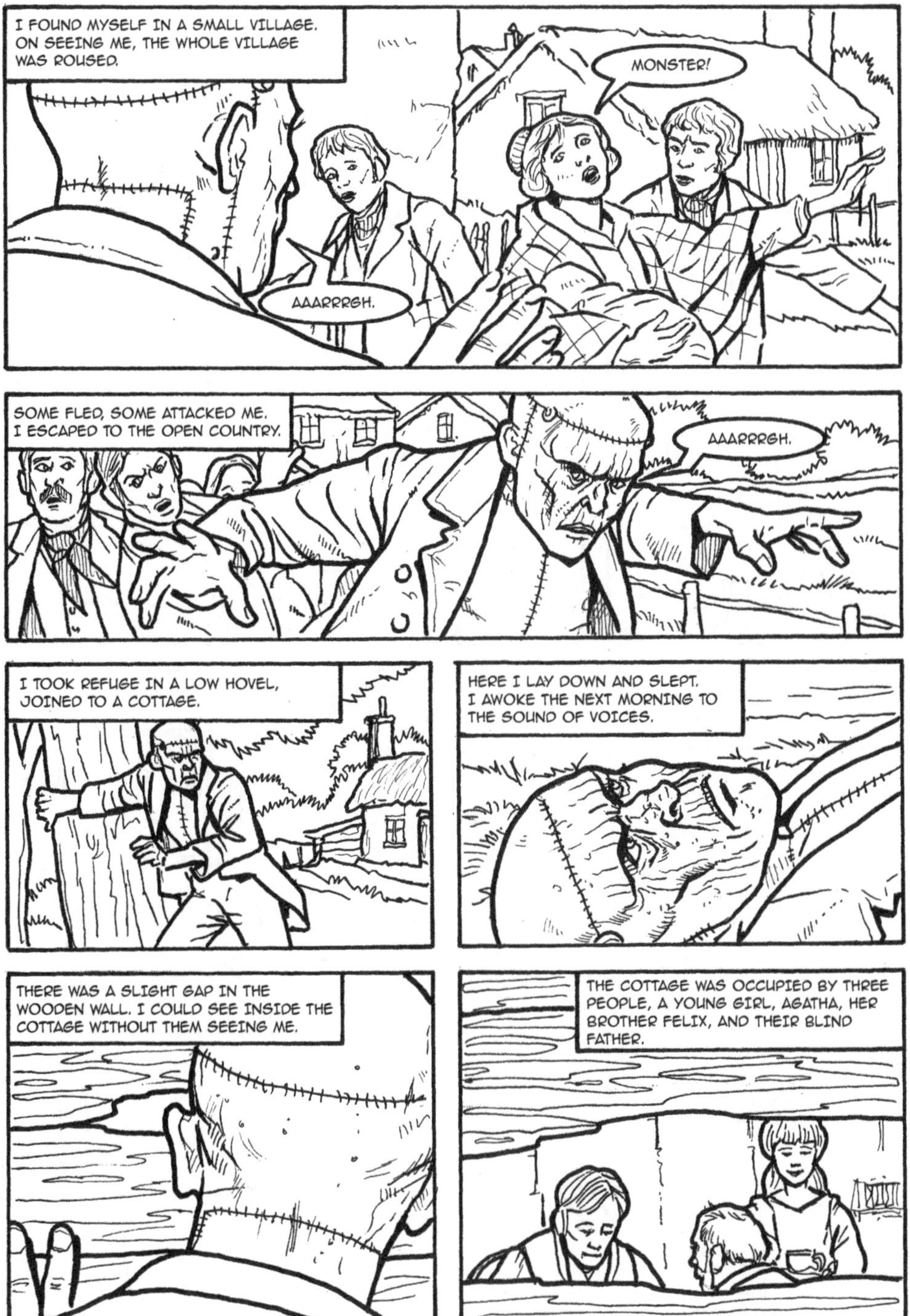
I FOUND MYSELF IN A SMALL VILLAGE. ON SEEING ME, THE WHOLE VILLAGE WAS ROUSED.
MONSTER!
AAARRRGH.
SOME FLED, SOME ATTACKED ME. I ESCAPED TO THE OPEN COUNTRY.
AAARRRGH.
I TOOK REFUGE IN A LOW HOVEL, JOINED TO A COTTAGE.
HERE I LAY DOWN AND SLEPT. I AWOKE THE NEXT MORNING TO THE SOUND OF VOICES.
THERE WAS A SLIGHT GAP IN THE WOODEN WALL. I COULD SEE INSIDE THE COTTAGE WITHOUT THEM SEEING ME.
THE COTTAGE WAS OCCUPIED BY THREE PEOPLE, A YOUNG GIRL, AGATHA, HER BROTHER FELIX, AND THEIR BLIND FATHER.

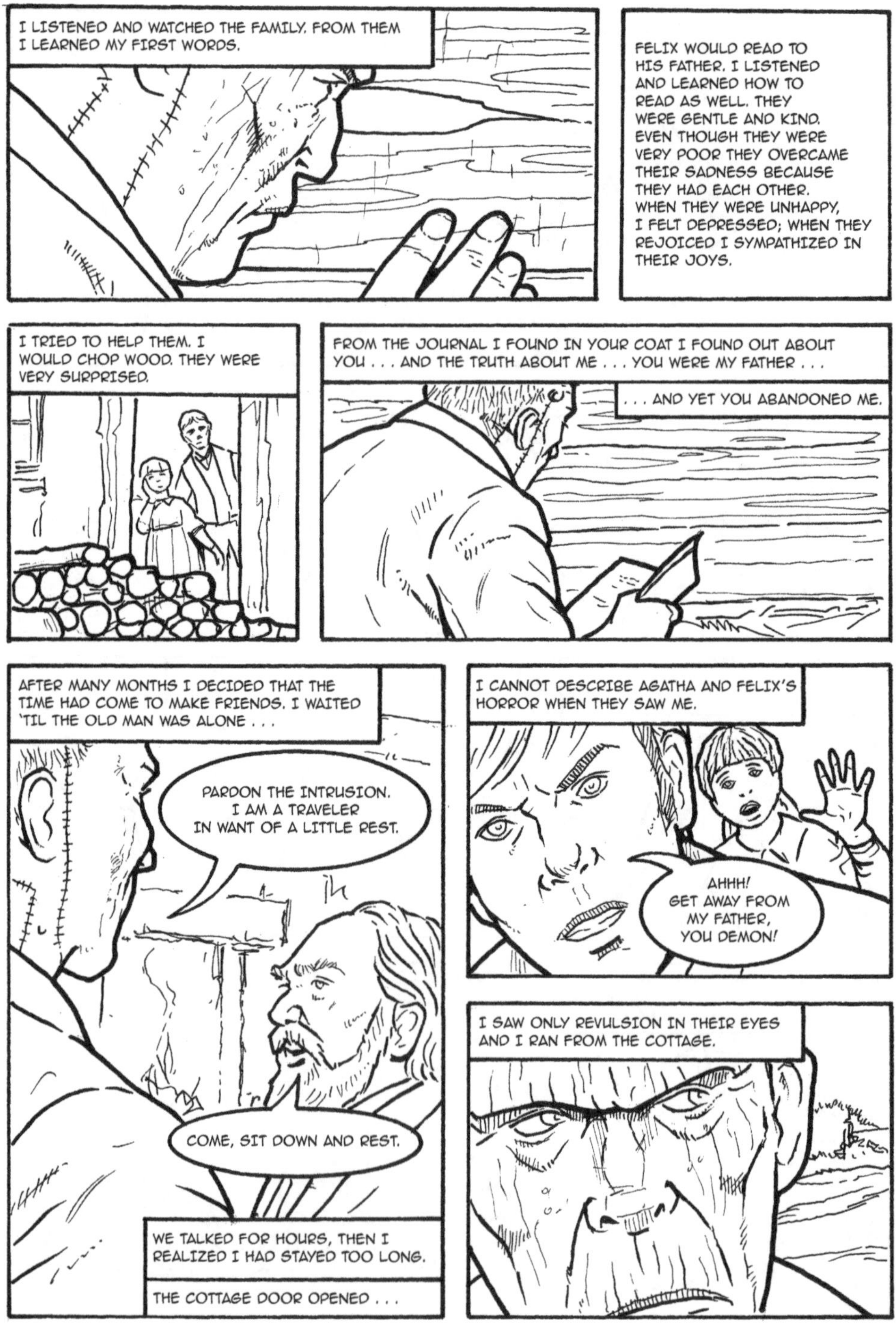
I LISTENED AND WATCHED THE FAMILY. FROM THEM I LEARNED MY FIRST WORDS.
FELIX WOULD READ TO HIS FATHER. I LISTENED AND LEARNED HOW TO READ AS WELL. THEY WERE GENTLE AND KIND. EVEN THOUGH THEY WERE VERY POOR THEY OVERCAME THEIR SADNESS BECAUSE THEY HAD EACH OTHER. WHEN THEY WERE UNHAPPY, I FELT DEPRESSED; WHEN THEY REJOICED I SYMPATHIZED IN THEIR JOYS.
I TRIED TO HELP THEM. I WOULD CHOP WOOD. THEY WERE VERY SURPRISED.
FROM THE JOURNAL I FOUND IN YOUR COAT I FOUND OUT ABOUT YOU . . . AND THE TRUTH ABOUT ME . . . YOU WERE MY FATHER . . .
. . . AND YET YOU ABANDONED ME.
AFTER MANY MONTHS I DECIDED THAT THE TIME HAD COME TO MAKE FRIENDS. I WAITED 'TIL THE OLD MAN WAS ALONE . . .
PARDON THE INTRUSION. I AM A TRAVELER IN WANT OF A LITTLE REST.
COME, SIT DOWN AND REST.
WE TALKED FOR HOURS, THEN I REALIZED I HAD STAYED TOO LONG.
THE COTTAGE DOOR OPENED . . .
I CANNOT DESCRIBE AGATHA AND FELIX'S HORROR WHEN THEY SAW ME.
AHHH! GET AWAY FROM MY FATHER, YOU DEMON!
I SAW ONLY REVULSION IN THEIR EYES AND I RAN FROM THE COTTAGE.

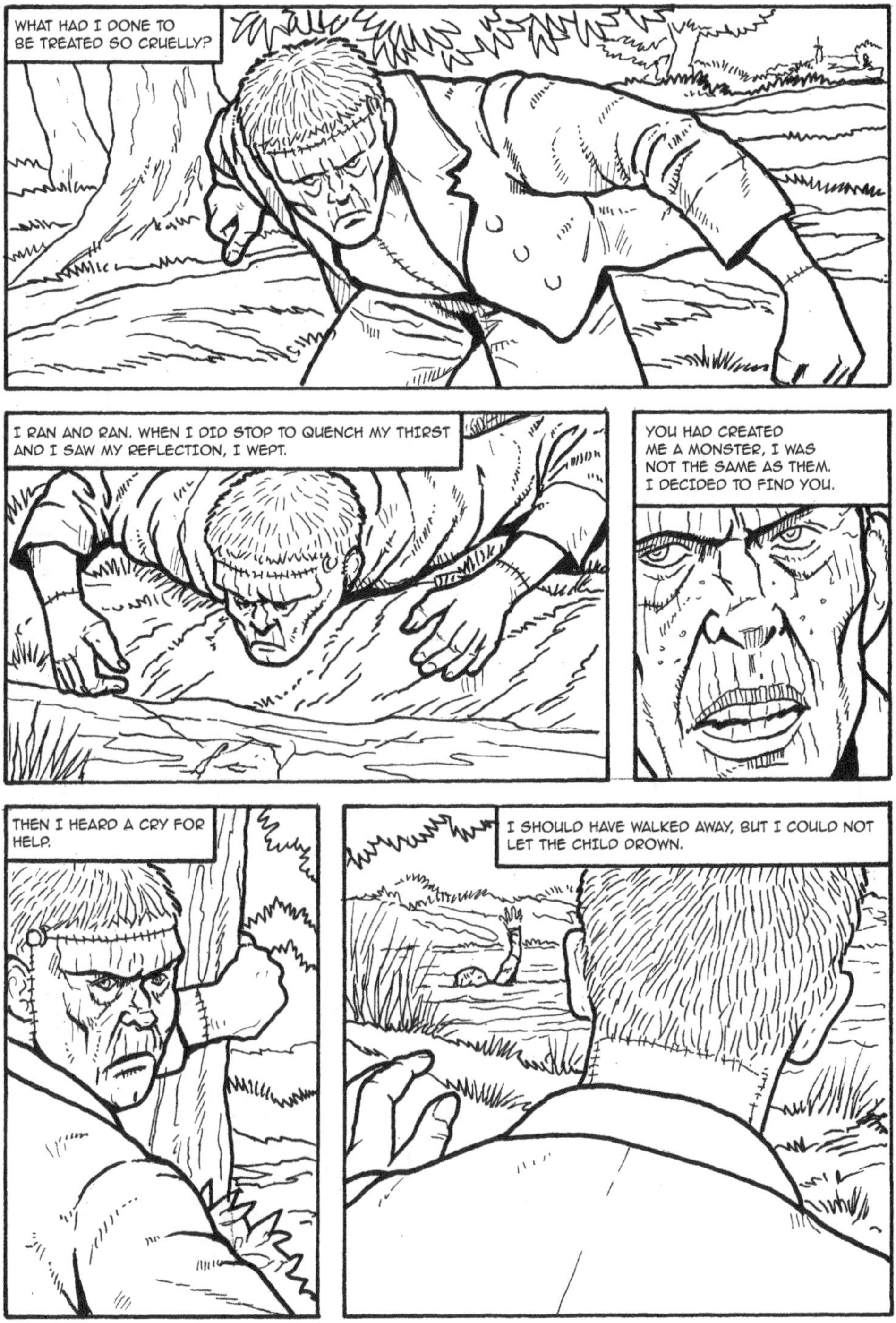
WHAT HAD I DONE TO BE TREATED SO CRUELLY?
I RAN AND RAN. WHEN I DID STOP TO QUENCH MY THIRST AND I SAW MY REFLECTION, I WEPT.
YOU HAD CREATED ME A MONSTER, I WAS NOT THE SAME AS THEM. I DECIDED TO FIND YOU.
THEN I HEARD A CRY FOR HELP.
I SHOULD HAVE WALKED AWAY, BUT I COULD NOT LET THE CHILD DROWN.

BUT I RECEIVED ONLY PAIN FOR MY ACTIONS.

GET AWAY FROM HER, YOU MONSTER!

AHHH!

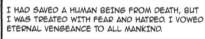

I HAD SAVED A HUMAN BEING FROM DEATH, BUT I WAS TREATED WITH FEAR AND HATRED. I VOWED ETERNAL VENGEANCE TO ALL MANKIND.

I CONTINUED MY JOURNEY. JUST OUTSIDE GENEVA I MET A SMALL BOY.

GO AWAY, YOU MONSTER, MY FATHER IS ALFONSE FRANKENSTEIN, AND HE WILL HAVE YOU PUNISHED.

I SEIZED THE BOY, HE STRUGGLED. MY HEART SWELLED WITH HELLISH TRIUMPH.

YOU ARE MY ENEMY!

I GRASPED HIS THROAT, AND IN A MOMENT HE LAY DEAD AT MY FEET.

YOU SHALL BE MY FIRST VICTIM!

I GAZED ON MY VICTIM, AND I WAS FILLED WITH EXULTATION. I KNEW THIS DEATH WOULD CARRY DESPAIR TO YOU.

AS I GAZED ON THE CHILD, I SAW SOMETHING GLITTERING ON HIS BREAST. I TOOK IT; IT WAS A LOCKET, A PORTRAIT OF A MOST LOVELY WOMAN; I REMEMBERED THAT I WAS DEPRIVED OF THE DELIGHTS THAT SUCH BEAUTIFUL CREATURES COULD BESTOW.

I LEFT THE SPOT WHERE I HAD COMMITTED MURDER.

I ENTERED A BARN, A WOMAN WAS ASLEEP IN THE STRAW.

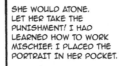

SHE WOULD ATONE. LET HER TAKE THE PUNISHMENT! I HAD LEARNED HOW TO WORK MISCHIEF. I PLACED THE PORTRAIT IN HER POCKET.

FOR SOME DAYS I HAUNTED THE SPOT WHERE THESE SCENES HAD TAKEN PLACE. IT WAS THEN WE FIRST MET. AT LENGTH I WANDERED TOWARD THESE MOUNTAINS, CONSUMED BY A BURNING PASSION ONLY YOU CAN GRATIFY . . .

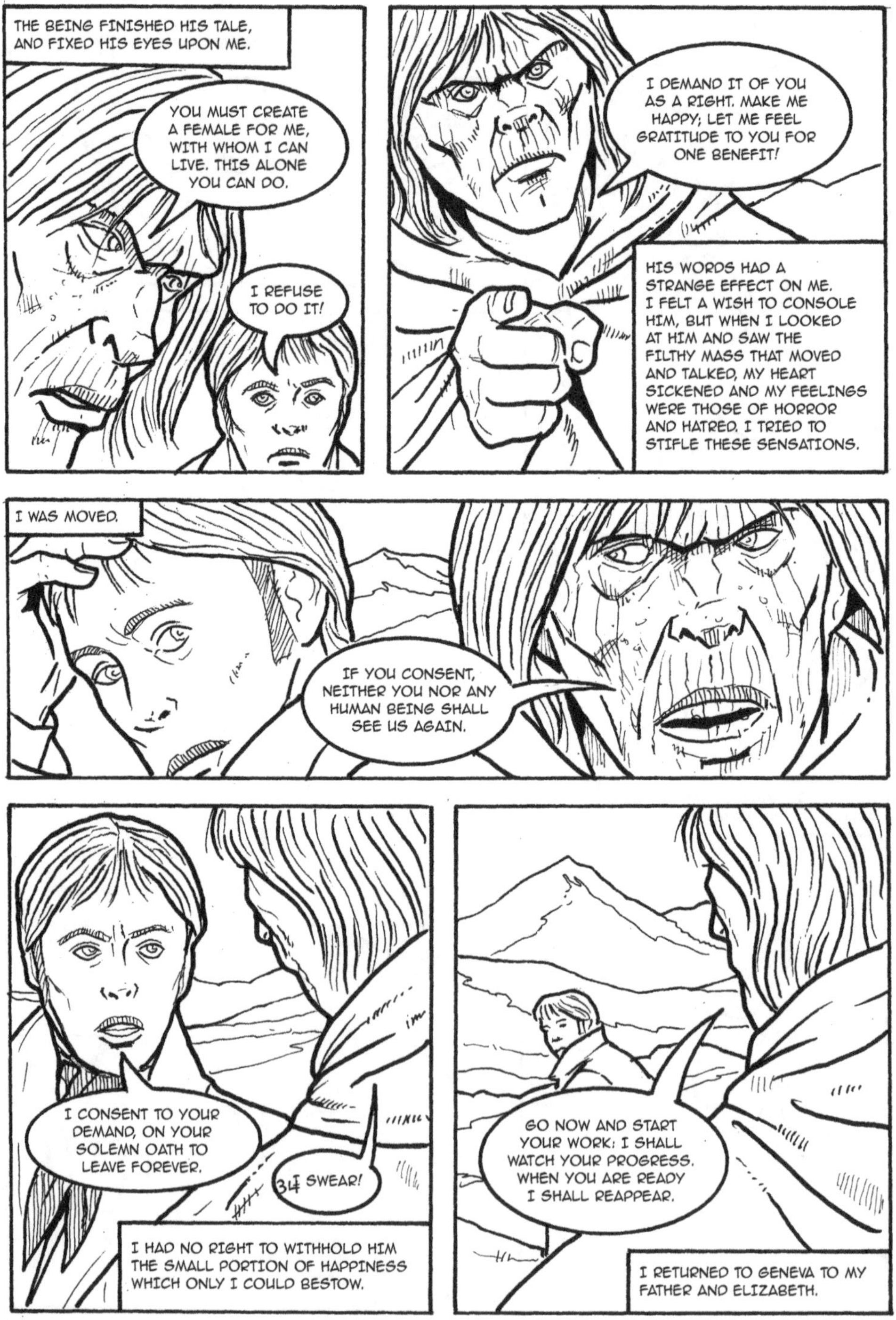
THE BEING FINISHED HIS TALE, AND FIXED HIS EYES UPON ME.
YOU MUST CREATE A FEMALE FOR ME, WITH WHOM I CAN LIVE. THIS ALONE YOU CAN DO.
I REFUSE TO DO IT!
I DEMAND IT OF YOU AS A RIGHT. MAKE ME HAPPY; LET ME FEEL GRATITUDE TO YOU FOR ONE BENEFIT!
HIS WORDS HAD A STRANGE EFFECT ON ME. I FELT A WISH TO CONSOLE HIM, BUT WHEN I LOOKED AT HIM AND SAW THE FILTHY MASS THAT MOVED AND TALKED, MY HEART SICKENED AND MY FEELINGS WERE THOSE OF HORROR AND HATRED. I TRIED TO STIFLE THESE SENSATIONS.
I WAS MOVED.
IF YOU CONSENT, NEITHER YOU NOR ANY HUMAN BEING SHALL SEE US AGAIN.
I CONSENT TO YOUR DEMAND, ON YOUR SOLEMN OATH TO LEAVE FOREVER.
I SWEAR!
I HAD NO RIGHT TO WITHHOLD HIM THE SMALL PORTION OF HAPPINESS WHICH ONLY I COULD BESTOW.
GO NOW AND START YOUR WORK: I SHALL WATCH YOUR PROGRESS. WHEN YOU ARE READY I SHALL REAPPEAR.
I RETURNED TO GENEVA TO MY FATHER AND ELIZABETH.

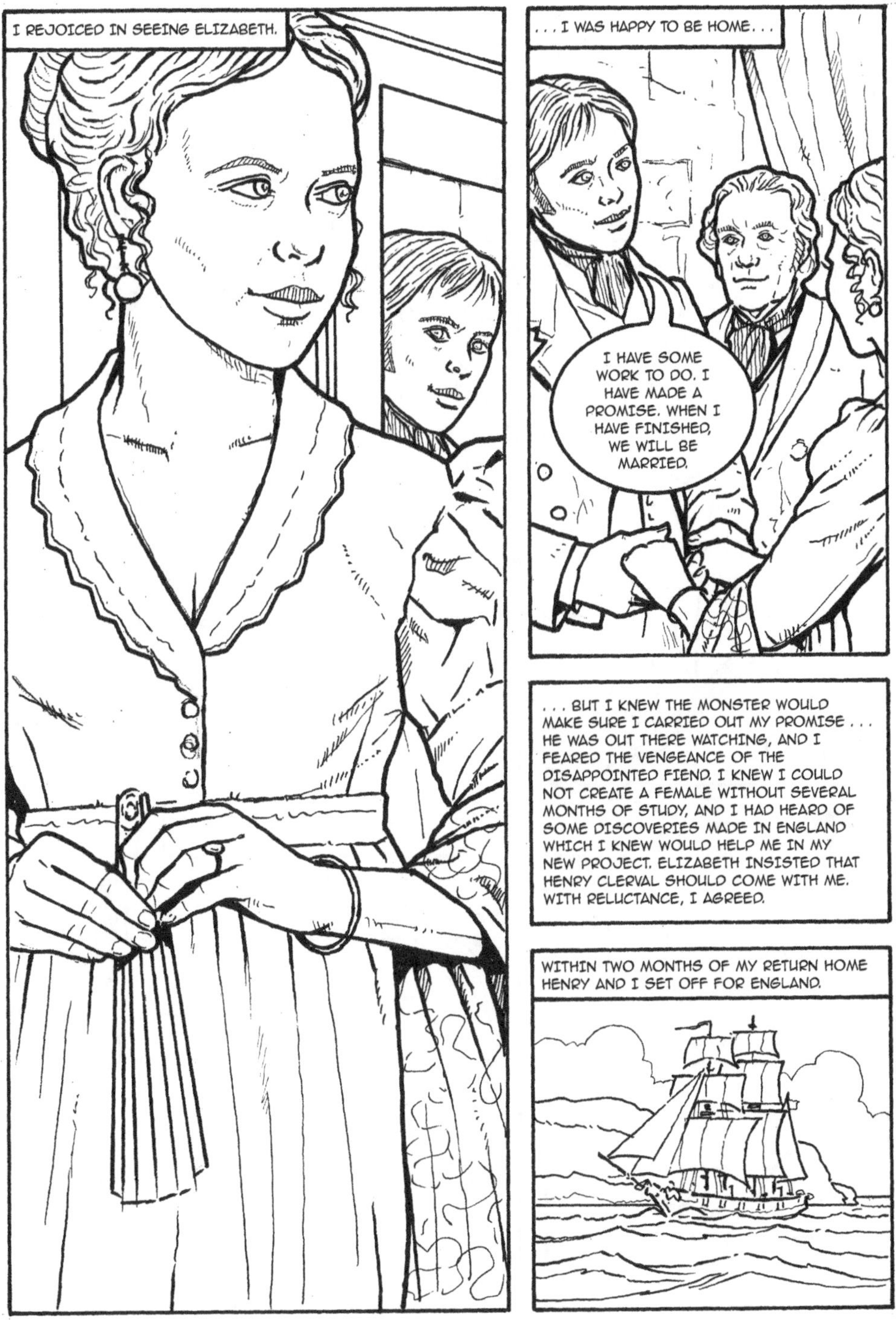
I REJOICED IN SEEING ELIZABETH.
. . . I WAS HAPPY TO BE HOME . . .
I HAVE SOME WORK TO DO. I HAVE MADE A PROMISE. WHEN I HAVE FINISHED, WE WILL BE MARRIED.
. . . BUT I KNEW THE MONSTER WOULD MAKE SURE I CARRIED OUT MY PROMISE . . . HE WAS OUT THERE WATCHING, AND I FEARED THE VENGEANCE OF THE DISAPPOINTED FIEND. I KNEW I COULD NOT CREATE A FEMALE WITHOUT SEVERAL MONTHS OF STUDY, AND I HAD HEARD OF SOME DISCOVERIES MADE IN ENGLAND WHICH I KNEW WOULD HELP ME IN MY NEW PROJECT. ELIZABETH INSISTED THAT HENRY CLERVAL SHOULD COME WITH ME. WITH RELUCTANCE, I AGREED.
WITHIN TWO MONTHS OF MY RETURN HOME HENRY AND I SET OFF FOR ENGLAND.

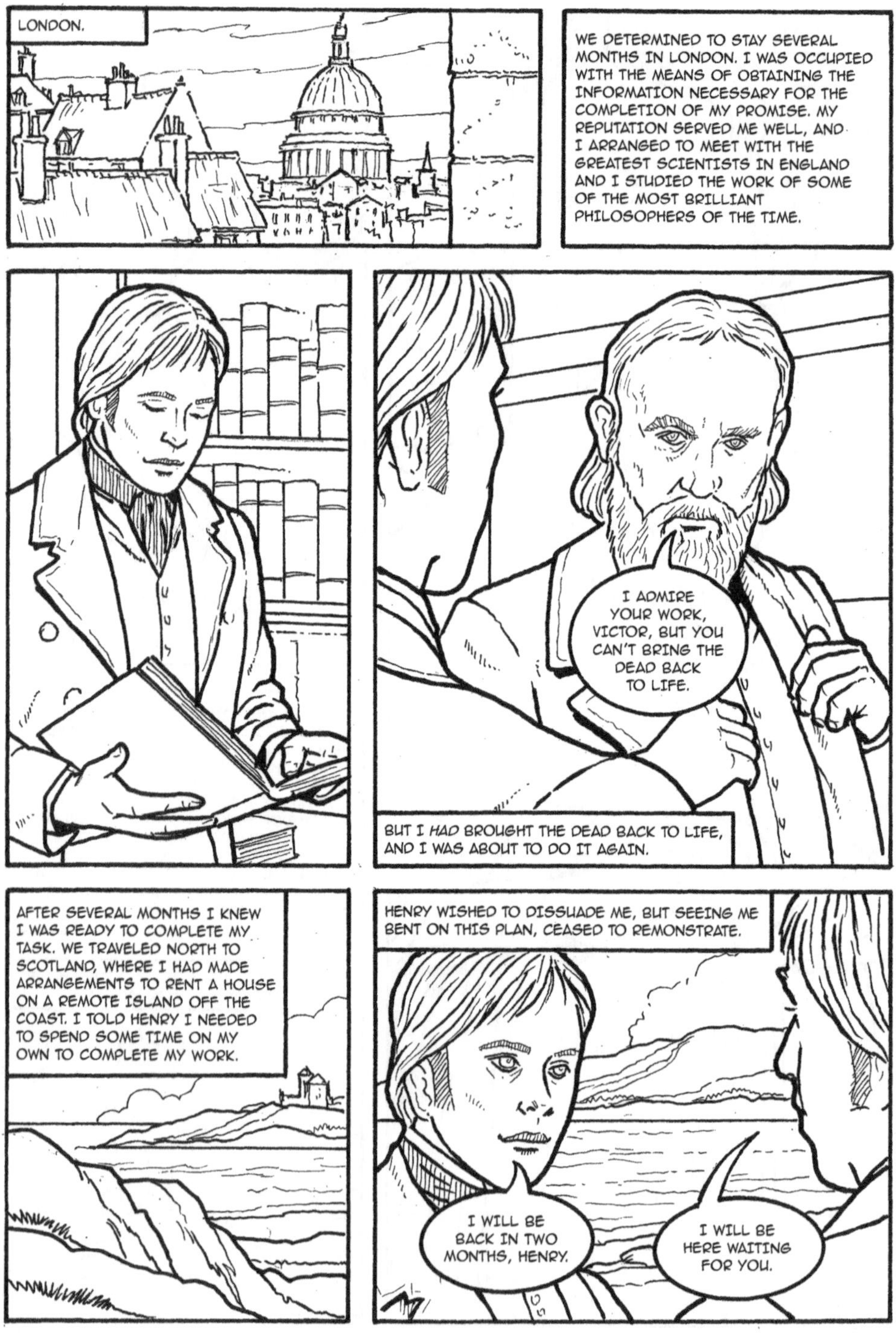
LONDON.
WE DETERMINED TO STAY SEVERAL MONTHS IN LONDON. I WAS OCCUPIED WITH THE MEANS OF OBTAINING THE INFORMATION NECESSARY FOR THE COMPLETION OF MY PROMISE. MY REPUTATION SERVED ME WELL, AND I ARRANGED TO MEET WITH THE GREATEST SCIENTISTS IN ENGLAND AND I STUDIED THE WORK OF SOME OF THE MOST BRILLIANT PHILOSOPHERS OF THE TIME.
I ADMIRE YOUR WORK, VICTOR, BUT YOU CAN'T BRING THE DEAD BACK TO LIFE.
BUT I *HAD* BROUGHT THE DEAD BACK TO LIFE, AND I WAS ABOUT TO DO IT AGAIN.
AFTER SEVERAL MONTHS I KNEW I WAS READY TO COMPLETE MY TASK. WE TRAVELED NORTH TO SCOTLAND, WHERE I HAD MADE ARRANGEMENTS TO RENT A HOUSE ON A REMOTE ISLAND OFF THE COAST. I TOLD HENRY I NEEDED TO SPEND SOME TIME ON MY OWN TO COMPLETE MY WORK.
HENRY WISHED TO DISSUADE ME, BUT SEEING ME BENT ON THIS PLAN, CEASED TO REMONSTRATE.
I WILL BE BACK IN TWO MONTHS, HENRY.
I WILL BE HERE WAITING FOR YOU.

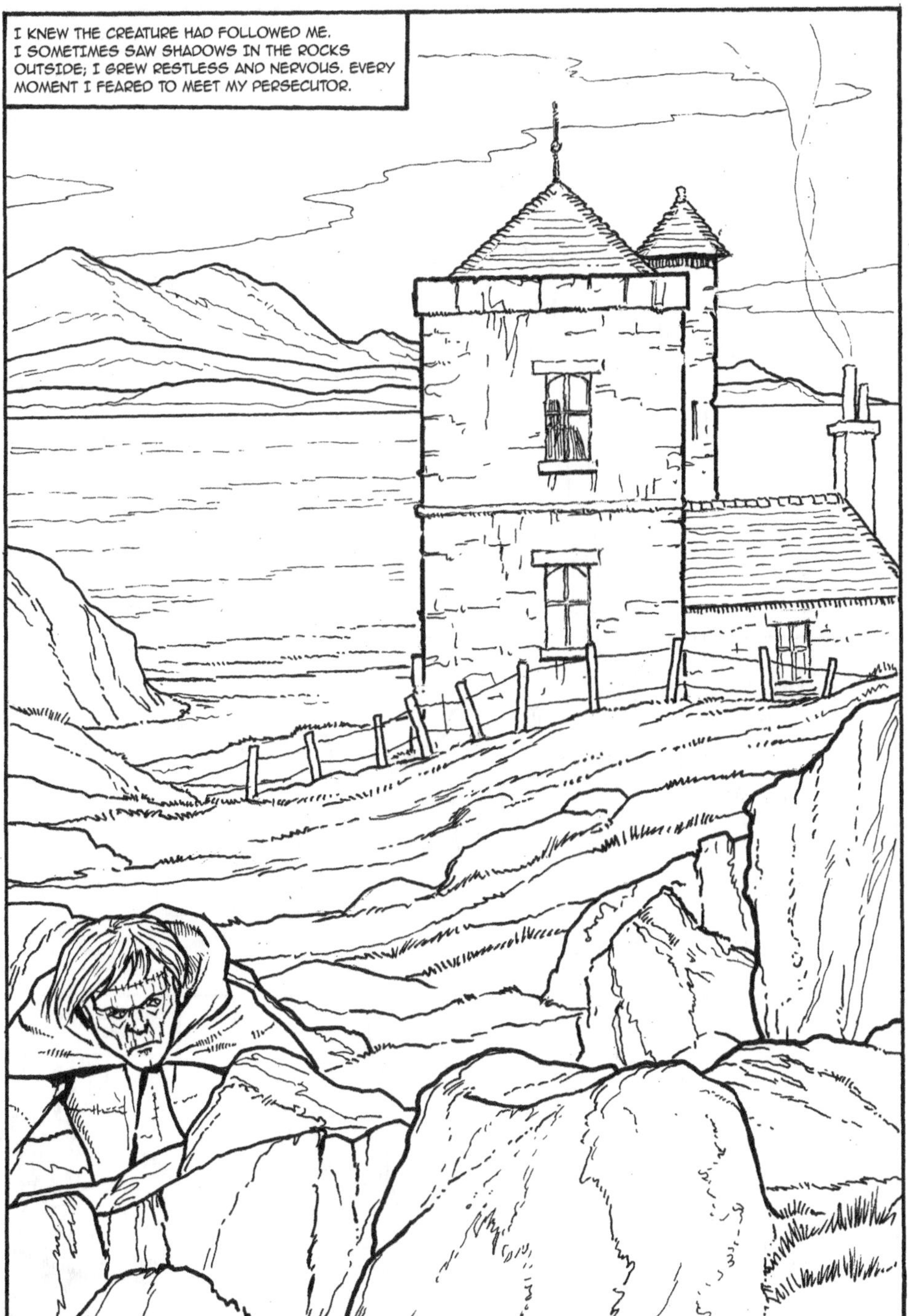
I KNEW THE CREATURE HAD FOLLOWED ME. I SOMETIMES SAW SHADOWS IN THE ROCKS OUTSIDE; I GREW RESTLESS AND NERVOUS. EVERY MOMENT I FEARED TO MEET MY PERSECUTOR.

I BEGAN TO CREATE MY NEW CREATURE. I NO LONGER HAD THE THRILL OF DISCOVERY TO PUSH ME ON, ONLY THE DREAD OF FAILURE.

I ASSEMBLED ALL THE PARTS. WEEKS PASSED AS I PUT TOGETHER THE BONES, ORGANS, MUSCLES, AND VEINS.

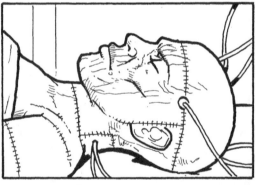

SHE WAS ALMOST FINISHED . . .

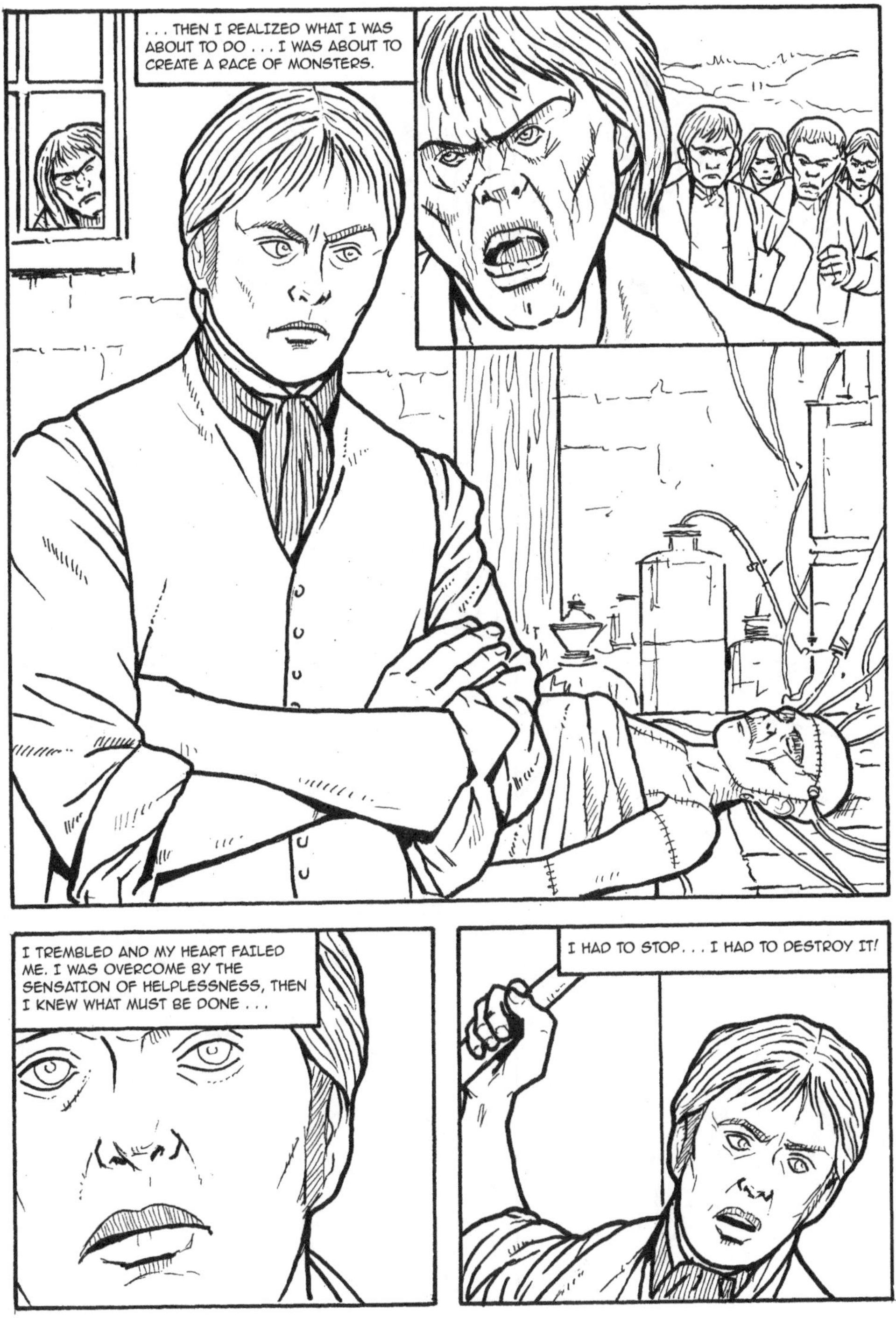
. . . THEN I REALIZED WHAT I WAS ABOUT TO DO . . . I WAS ABOUT TO CREATE A RACE OF MONSTERS.
I TREMBLED AND MY HEART FAILED ME. I WAS OVERCOME BY THE SENSATION OF HELPLESSNESS, THEN I KNEW WHAT MUST BE DONE . . .
I HAD TO STOP. . . I HAD TO DESTROY IT!

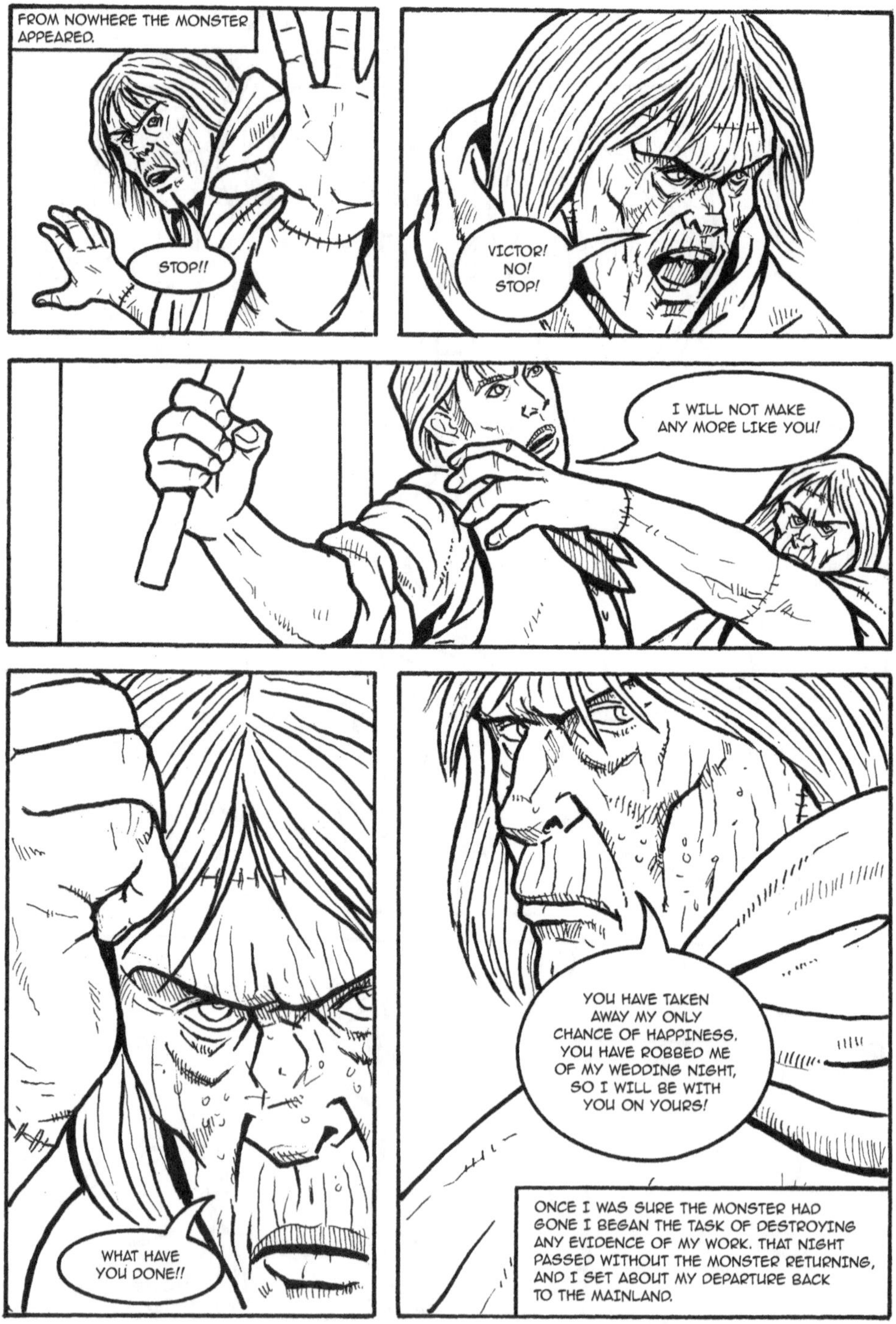
FROM NOWHERE THE MONSTER APPEARED.
STOP!!
VICTOR! NO! STOP!
I WILL NOT MAKE ANY MORE LIKE YOU!
WHAT HAVE YOU DONE!!
YOU HAVE TAKEN AWAY MY ONLY CHANCE OF HAPPINESS. YOU HAVE ROBBED ME OF MY WEDDING NIGHT, SO I WILL BE WITH YOU ON YOURS!
ONCE I WAS SURE THE MONSTER HAD GONE I BEGAN THE TASK OF DESTROYING ANY EVIDENCE OF MY WORK. THAT NIGHT PASSED WITHOUT THE MONSTER RETURNING, AND I SET ABOUT MY DEPARTURE BACK TO THE MAINLAND.

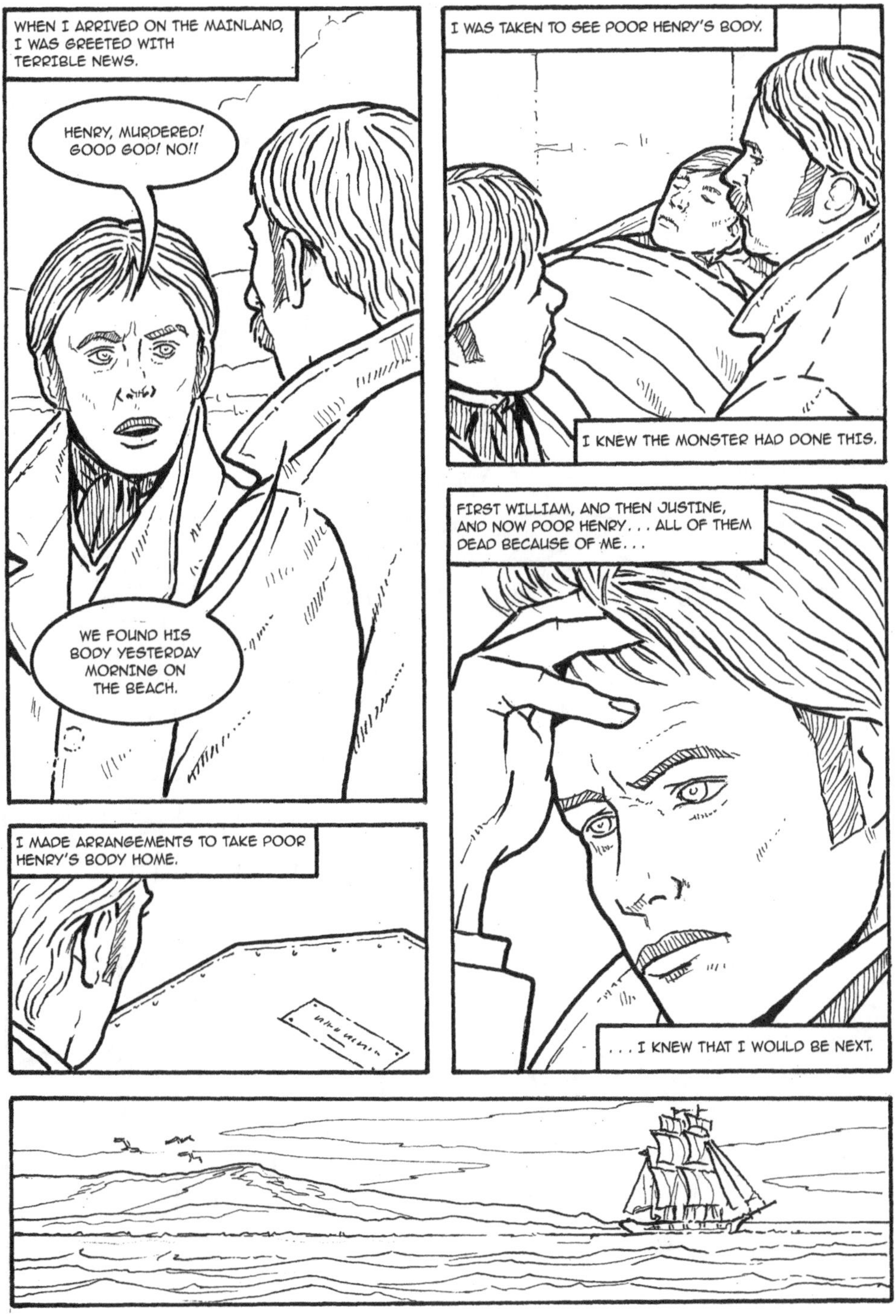
WHEN I ARRIVED ON THE MAINLAND, I WAS GREETED WITH TERRIBLE NEWS.
HENRY, MURDERED! GOOD GOD! NO!!
WE FOUND HIS BODY YESTERDAY MORNING ON THE BEACH.
I WAS TAKEN TO SEE POOR HENRY'S BODY.
I KNEW THE MONSTER HAD DONE THIS.
I MADE ARRANGEMENTS TO TAKE POOR HENRY'S BODY HOME.
FIRST WILLIAM, AND THEN JUSTINE, AND NOW POOR HENRY. . . ALL OF THEM DEAD BECAUSE OF ME. . .
. . . I KNEW THAT I WOULD BE NEXT.

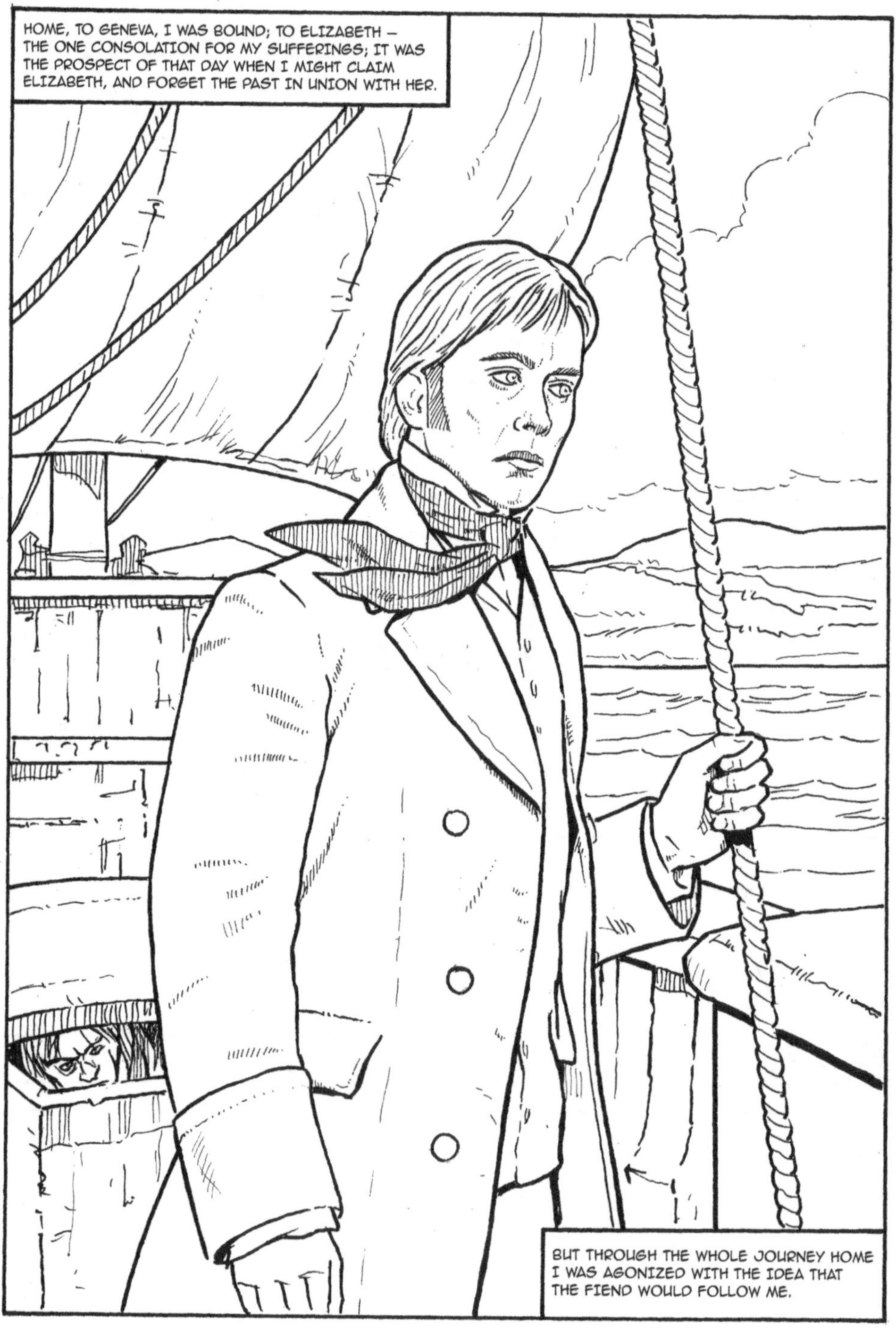
HOME, TO GENEVA, I WAS BOUND; TO ELIZABETH – THE ONE CONSOLATION FOR MY SUFFERINGS; IT WAS THE PROSPECT OF THAT DAY WHEN I MIGHT CLAIM ELIZABETH, AND FORGET THE PAST IN UNION WITH HER.
BUT THROUGH THE WHOLE JOURNEY HOME I WAS AGONIZED WITH THE IDEA THAT THE FIEND WOULD FOLLOW ME.

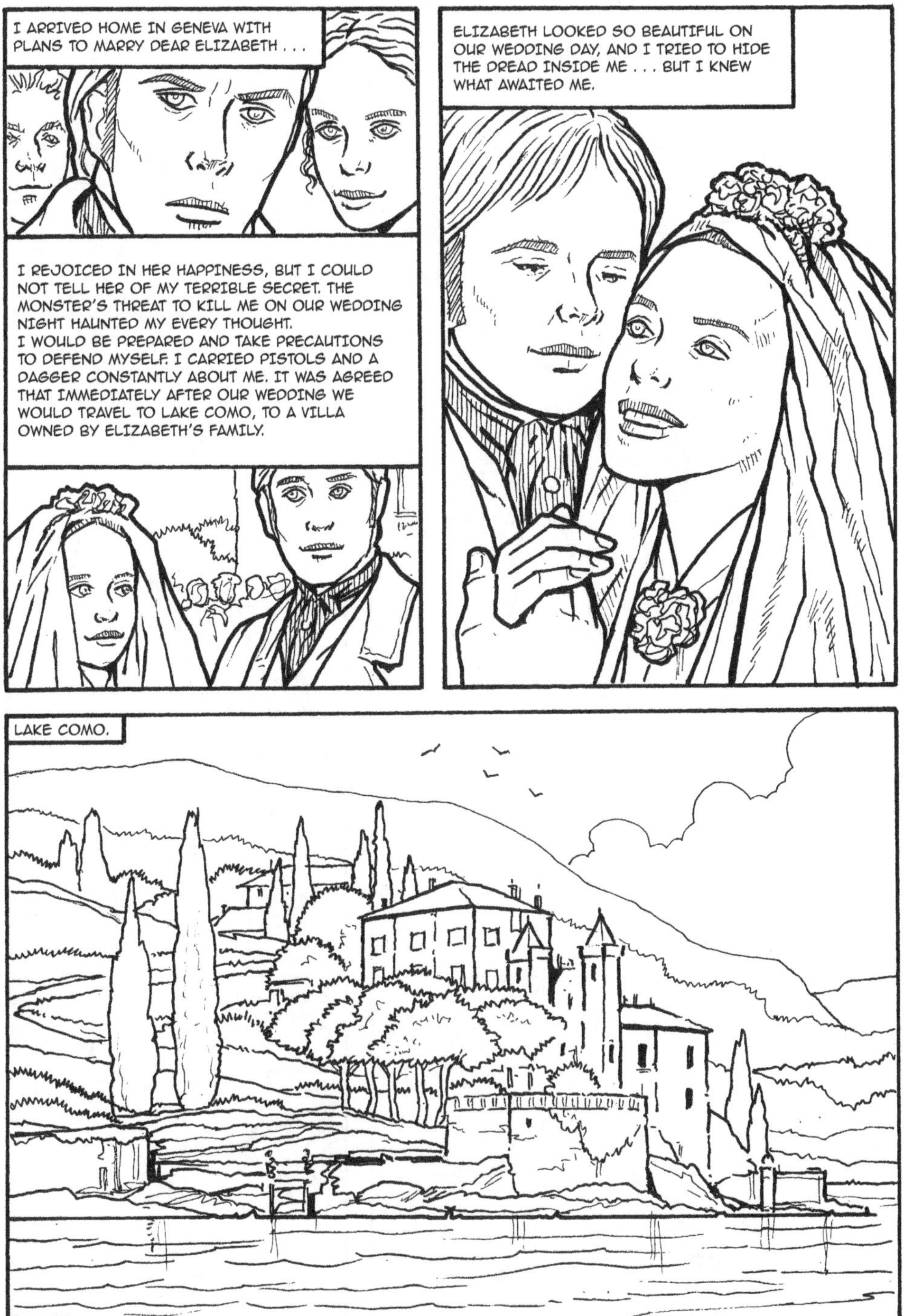
I ARRIVED HOME IN GENEVA WITH PLANS TO MARRY DEAR ELIZABETH . . .
ELIZABETH LOOKED SO BEAUTIFUL ON OUR WEDDING DAY, AND I TRIED TO HIDE THE DREAD INSIDE ME . . . BUT I KNEW WHAT AWAITED ME.
I REJOICED IN HER HAPPINESS, BUT I COULD NOT TELL HER OF MY TERRIBLE SECRET. THE MONSTER'S THREAT TO KILL ME ON OUR WEDDING NIGHT HAUNTED MY EVERY THOUGHT.
I WOULD BE PREPARED AND TAKE PRECAUTIONS TO DEFEND MYSELF. I CARRIED PISTOLS AND A DAGGER CONSTANTLY ABOUT ME. IT WAS AGREED THAT IMMEDIATELY AFTER OUR WEDDING WE WOULD TRAVEL TO LAKE COMO, TO A VILLA OWNED BY ELIZABETH'S FAMILY.
LAKE COMO.

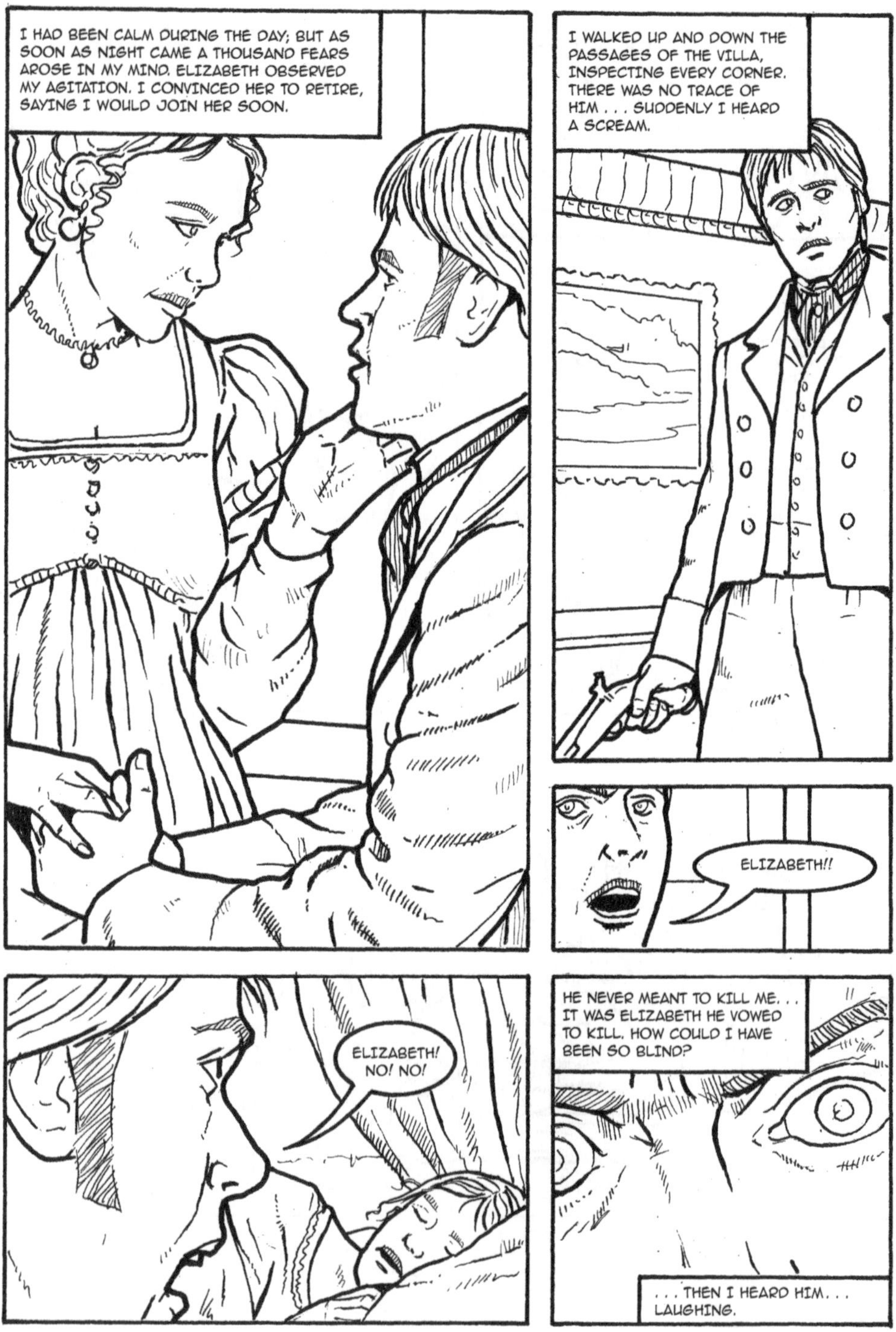
I HAD BEEN CALM DURING THE DAY; BUT AS SOON AS NIGHT CAME A THOUSAND FEARS AROSE IN MY MIND. ELIZABETH OBSERVED MY AGITATION. I CONVINCED HER TO RETIRE, SAYING I WOULD JOIN HER SOON.
I WALKED UP AND DOWN THE PASSAGES OF THE VILLA, INSPECTING EVERY CORNER. THERE WAS NO TRACE OF HIM . . . SUDDENLY I HEARD A SCREAM.
ELIZABETH!!
ELIZABETH! NO! NO!
HE NEVER MEANT TO KILL ME. . . IT WAS ELIZABETH HE VOWED TO KILL. HOW COULD I HAVE BEEN SO BLIND?
. . . THEN I HEARD HIM. . . LAUGHING.

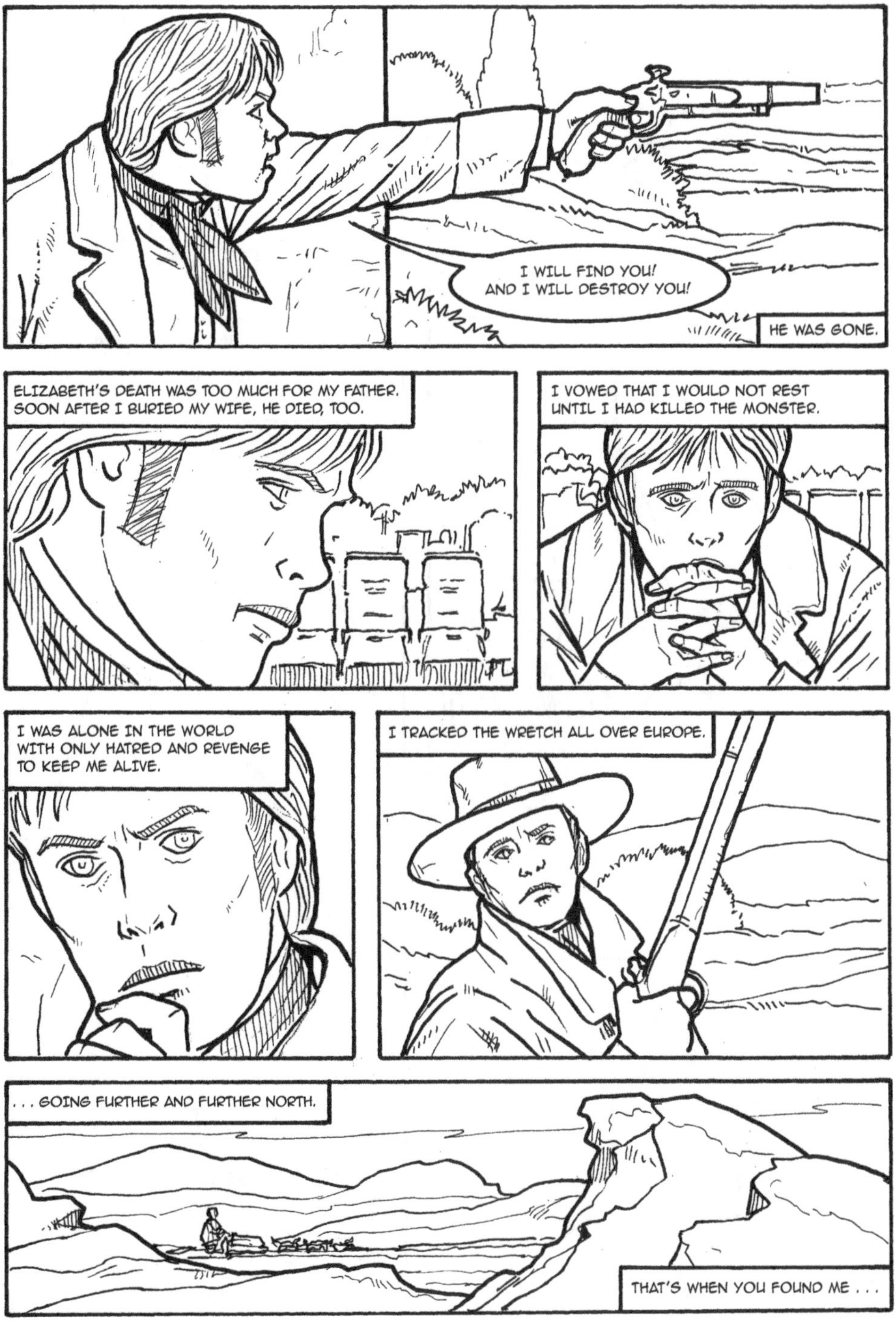
I WILL FIND YOU!
AND I WILL DESTROY YOU!
HE WAS GONE.
ELIZABETH'S DEATH WAS TOO MUCH FOR MY FATHER. SOON AFTER I BURIED MY WIFE, HE DIED, TOO.
I VOWED THAT I WOULD NOT REST UNTIL I HAD KILLED THE MONSTER.
I WAS ALONE IN THE WORLD WITH ONLY HATRED AND REVENGE TO KEEP ME ALIVE.
I TRACKED THE WRETCH ALL OVER EUROPE.
. . . GOING FURTHER AND FURTHER NORTH.
THAT'S WHEN YOU FOUND ME . . .

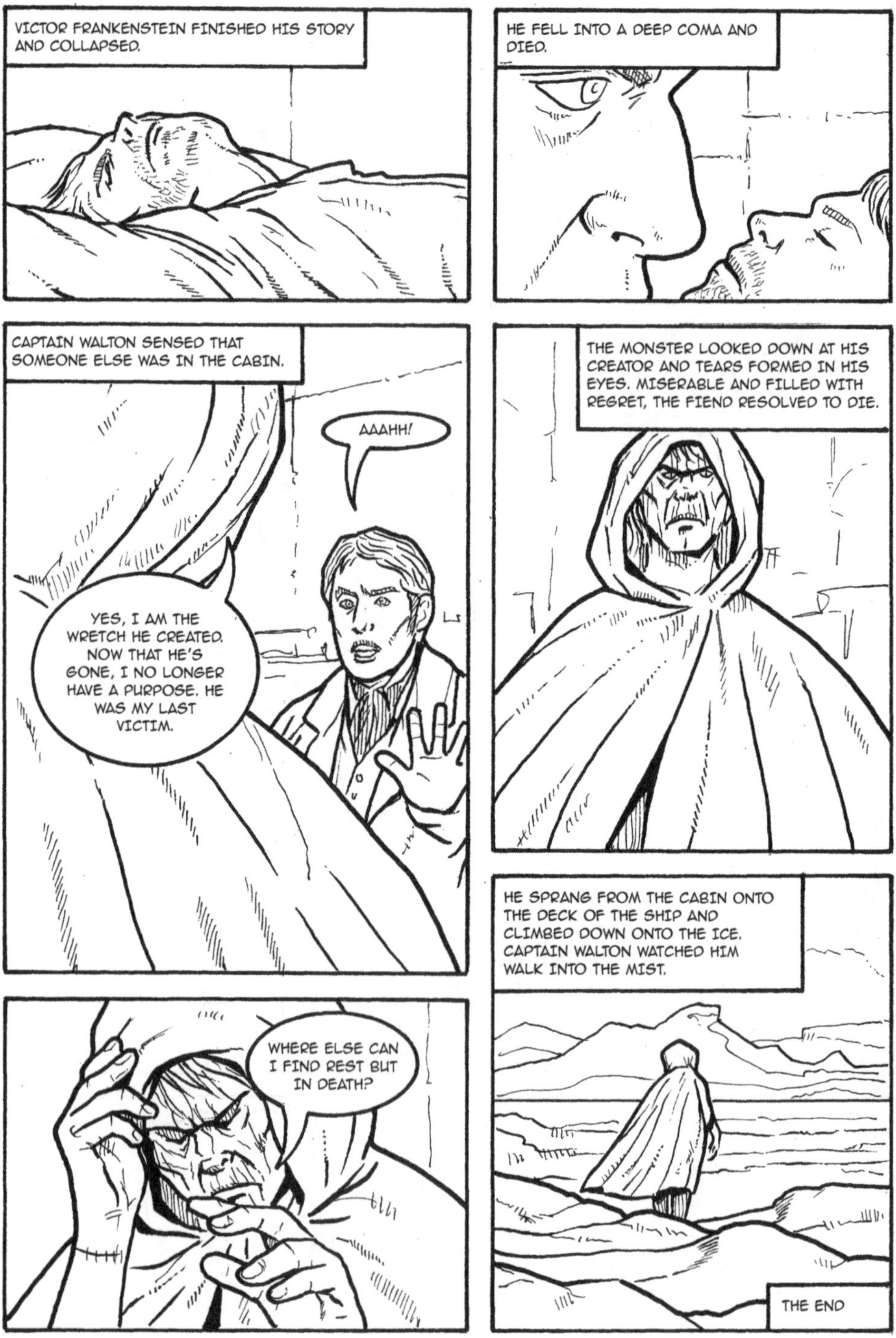
VICTOR FRANKENSTEIN FINISHED HIS STORY AND COLLAPSED.
HE FELL INTO A DEEP COMA AND DIED.
CAPTAIN WALTON SENSED THAT SOMEONE ELSE WAS IN THE CABIN.
AAAHH!
YES, I AM THE WRETCH HE CREATED. NOW THAT HE'S GONE, I NO LONGER HAVE A PURPOSE. HE WAS MY LAST VICTIM.
THE MONSTER LOOKED DOWN AT HIS CREATOR AND TEARS FORMED IN HIS EYES. MISERABLE AND FILLED WITH REGRET, THE FIEND RESOLVED TO DIE.
WHERE ELSE CAN I FIND REST BUT IN DEATH?
HE SPRANG FROM THE CABIN ONTO THE DECK OF THE SHIP AND CLIMBED DOWN ONTO THE ICE. CAPTAIN WALTON WATCHED HIM WALK INTO THE MIST.
THE END